John Polhemus

My First Vacation and Welcome Home

With a Brief Biographical Sketch

John Polhemus

My First Vacation and Welcome Home
With a Brief Biographical Sketch

ISBN/EAN: 9783337078546

Printed in Europe, USA, Canada, Australia, Japan

Cover: Foto ©Andreas Hilbeck / pixelio.de

More available books at **www.hansebooks.com**

Yours truly
John Polhemus

A Family Souvenir.

MY FIRST VACATION

AND

WELCOME HOME,

WITH A

BRIEF BIOGRAPHICAL SKETCH.

NEW YORK:
JOHN POLHEMUS PRINTING COMPANY.

1891.

AFTER an extended trip abroad covering a period of four months, a dinner was tendered to Mr. JOHN POLHEMUS, on his return, by his friends and associates in the Typothetæ, the Master-Printers' Society. The invitation was given on their behalf by R. Harmer Smith, Esq., Chairman, and Henry Bessey, Esq., James W. Pratt, Esq., James A. Rogers, Esq., and J. Faulkner, Esq., members of the Executive Committee. Mr. E. Parke Coby, the Secretary of the Society, completed the arrangements for the occasion, which was fixed at Hotel Martin, University Place, on Tuesday evening, September 22, 1891.

The dinner was handsomely served. Three long halls were joined together, in the rearmost a band of music being placed. Upon the arrival of Mr. Polhemus from his home in Flushing, and his greeting by those assembled, he was escorted to the table by Mr. Theodore L. De Vinne, the President of the Typothetæ, who took his place at the head of the board. Mr. Polhemus sat at his right, and Mr. Douglas Taylor on his left. A diagram of the table is as follows:

John Polhemus.   † Theo. L. De Vinne.   Douglas Taylor.

Capt. Jas. Parker. +   † W. C. Rogers.

Howard Lockwood.	J. J. Little.
Edw. Taylor.	R. Harmer Smith.
T. B. De Vinne.	J. W. Pratt.
H. G. Polhemus.	Henry Bessey.
H. Steenken.	Peter De Baun.
S. R. Walker.	C. Urquhart.
P. Bresnan.	W. W. Pasko.
Wm. Hubbard.	R. Nelson.
Rich'd Ridge.	Chas. H. Nicoll.
Chauncey Holt.	John H. Roy.
J. Faulkner.	Andrew Little.
F. E. Fitch.	Chas. T. Polhemus.
T. S. DeWolfe.	P. F. McBreen.
D. H. Gildersleeve.	L. Middleditch.
A. R. Hart.	M. M. Gilliss.
T. R. Hopkins.	L. D. Gallison.
W. F. Waters.	Homer Lee.
Jno. C. Rankin, Jr.	Wm. J. Pell.
L. G. Burgess.	James A. Rogers.

E. Parke Coby.

COMPLIMENTARY DINNER

TO

MR. JOHN POLHEMUS.

Menu.

Sauterne.

HUITRES BLUEPOINTS.

HORS-D'ŒUVRES VARIÉS.

Potages.

BISQUE DE HOMARD.

CONSOMMÉ PRINCESSE.

Poisson.

St. Julien.

FILETS DE STRIPED BASS À LA MARGUERY.

POMMES À L'ANGLAISE.

Entrées.

BOUCHÉES MONGLAS.

FILET DE BŒUF À LA PARISIENNE.

Legumes.

PETITS POIS.   CAROTTES NOUVELLES.

HARICOTS VERTS.   POMMES CHÂTEAU.

SPAGHETTI À L'ITALIENNE.

Rôti.

Roderer "Extra Cuvée,"

GROUSE RÔTIE AU CRESSON.

SALADE DE SAISON.

Entremets.

GLACE FANTAISIE BISCUITS.

TARTE AUX AMANDES.

FROMAGES.   FRUITS.   MOKA.

AFTER DINNER REMARKS.

After coffee was served, Mr. DE VINNE called the assemblage to order. He said:

GENTLEMEN AND BROTHERS OF THE TYPOTHETÆ: I am much pleased to see our Society so well represented this evening. It proves that the occasion which brings us together is one of interest to all. I think it a privilege that by your favor I have been asked to sit at this table, with our good friend on my right, and to testify to our regard for him as a faithful member of our Society, and to voice our appreciation of his worth as a man. I do this all the more heartily because my relations with Mr. Polhemus have been more personal than official. He is, indeed, an old friend. Mark Twain once said that he had a wood pile between his house and that of a neighbor; the wood pile had been there for many years, yet he and the neighbor were excellent friends. That is our position. The wood pile has never been a cause of dissension.

Forty years ago we were working very near each other, on opposite corners of Cortlandt and Washington streets. He was a newly-launched master printer. I was foreman in the office of Francis Hart & Co. I then had good opportunity to see and

learn how hard it was for a new comer to get and keep a foot-
hold among master printers. New York was then a comparatively small city, not one-third of its present size; there was
not much work to be done, and the rates for competitive work
were low. There was as much competition then as there is
now. Labor saving machinery was just coming into use, but at
that time it gave little benefit to the job printer. The average
compositor or pressman was not well trained, and was rather
more dissipated and irregular in his attendance than he is now.
In his fight for success, the young master printer had to rely
more on his own arms and on his own wits than on those of
his workmen. The more difficult parts of the work the master
printer had to do himself. No one then thought of the eight-
hour or even nine-hour day. For most days in the year ten
hours was not enough. How often, at late hours of the night,
have I looked out of the windows of our office and seen the
lights flaming in the office of Polhemus & de Vries, and I knew
they were sure to be there until long after daybreak. These
late hours were not of choice, but of necessity. The young master
printer had to take the work that he could get, and not the work
that he would like. If he could not get work to be done by day,
he must take that which had to be done at night.

After fifteen years of this kind of work, Mr. Polhemus rightly
thought that he was qualified for better work than catalogues
printed at night. He thought, too, that Cortlandt street was
too narrow a field; so he moved his office to the classical neighborhood of Ann and Nassau streets. He went where there was
then the most work to be done. He went to put himself in
the thick of the fight of competition. I do not know whether
he was induced to go there by recollections of the late Daniel

Fanshaw, whose august presence and heavily-frilled shirt bosom seemed good evidences of material prosperity, or whether he had looked with aspiring eyes on the gorgeous equipage of Jonas Winchester, who, some time before, had his office a little further down the street, and who used to come rattling down to that office in a carriage with liveried driver and footman. Perhaps not. His disregard for show and pretense forbids the supposition. He must have gone to Ann street because it was then the "High 'Change" of printers, and he was bound to have a seat in the front.

I will not attempt to follow his fortunes there. It is enough to say that he had his share of the calamities of business. He suffered more than ordinary loss from fraudulent buyers. Twice he was burnt out, and he had more than his share of conflicts with workmen.

Of the latter I will briefly speak. I have no desire to rake the ashes of quarrels that are dead and buried, but it seems necessary to allude to them, for it was in these fires that the strong points of his character were to be seen.

About five years ago, our Typothetæ entertained a complaint from Typographical Union No. 6 that the compositors of this city were not getting their rightful share of the proceeds of their labor. This was coupled with an unusually short notice that we must pay more for piece composition. Of evidence to justify this complaint and this demand the Union had none whatever. Nor were the delegates of the Union in a mood to listen to our explanation of the condition of the printing business. They wanted more pay and they must have it. We deliberated and said, "The price is unreasonably high, but as an experiment we will pay it." This was not enough. The Union

officials wanted, to use their expression, " more power." In
other words, they wanted to drive out of our offices every man
who did not belong to their Union, irrespective of the objec-
tionable man's age or merit. The master printers should not
be allowed to employ any man who did not belong to their
society. We might be nominally at the head of our business,
but the real government of the house was to be vested in the
"chairman of the chapel." who was to carry out the orders of
the officials of the Union. The Union claimed to be four
thousand strong, to have a full treasury, a powerful backing
from affiliated Trades Unions, and to be strong enough to en-
force any demand.

Our Typothetæ said to this last demand, " We shall not submit." So we had a strike. It was a thorough strike, for it took
out of our offices not only piece compositors and time hands,
but pressmen and electrotypers.

One of the offices picked out for special attack by the strikers
was that of John Polhemus. Like many of us. he fortified himself in his deserted office, and resisted the men who would neither
work themselves nor let others take their places. So wisely and
so bravely did he manage his affairs, that at the end of the strike
he had no need of the repentant mutineers who wanted to return. Their places had been filled with better men. The Union
officials requested that the old men be taken back, but no
wheedling or threats on the part of the Union could induce Mr.
Polhemus to displace the men who had stood by him. He had
but one answer : " I have given my word to the new men that
they shall not be displaced, and I shall keep my promise."
Then began retaliation. Mr. Polhemus's name was struck off
the roll of Union offices. It was put under ban. No Union man

would be allowed thereafter to work for him. These hostilities did not make him change his purpose.

Then a new method of worrying—the Irish boycott—was applied. Mr. Polhemus's customers were notified that they must send no more work to his office. If they did, they, too, would be boycotted.

In due time came an official representing a great political party that was then having much work done in Mr. Polhemus's office, who said to Mr. Polhemus in substance : " We like you, your work and your prices, but we do not like your antagonism to the Typographical Union. It is damaging to us as a party. We beg you to make peace with the Union. If you do not, we shall certainly take our work away. We cannot afford to incur their hostility."

The answer of Mr. Polhemus was quick and to the point. " My antagonism to the Union is of its own seeking, not mine. I shall not change my plans. If you cannot afford to risk its hostility, I can. You may take your work away. I lived without it before, and I can live without it hereafter." (Loud applause.)

The work did go and his income was damaged, but John Polhemus soon found other work to take its place. He did live without it, and he still prospers.

I do not want to be prolix, but I beg time for a short digression. There is a deal of cant afloat about the sordidness of trade. There is a notion that a trader or mechanic will submit to great injustices and will descend to much meanness rather than lose money, or an opportunity to make money. There is a belief that the men of principle, of high ideals and unselfish action are largely men of leisure, who were never in trade. I do not so read history. The master-weavers of Flanders, the traders of the German Rhine, the master mechanics of London, are examples

of the men who really began the practical work for the establishment of civil rights. As a class they have done the most and
suffered the most for liberty. The old spirit is still strong. I say
here that John Polhemus, in standing up for the equal rights of
all compositors to a chance to earn a living, and in refusing to
proscribe a majority of the printers of the country, has done good
service to the trade and to the cause of personal liberty. I am
very sure that the men who threatened him with the destruction
of his business are now convinced that he has clear convictions
of right and wrong, that he obeys these convictions at any sacri-
fice, and that he values his own self-respect more than money.
(Applause.) I think, too, that the man who took his work away
is also well convinced by this time that he sells printing only, and
does not sell his principles. (Applause.) In this matter John
Polhemus fought a good fight. He has kept the faith and shown
the courage of his Dutch ancestors.

I should do an injustice if I failed to speak of all Mr. Polhemus's services to our art in another direction. Whoever has been
in his office could not fail to note the skill he has shown with the
management of his material. I do not believe there is another
office in the country in which so much work is done in so small
space, without crowding the workmen. (Applause.) The " Polhemus cases, chases and quoins " are labor saving devices which
show his thorough understanding of the needs of his art and of
his love for that art. He has done admirable work. If there is a
better piece of table work in a book than that in his " Lloyds
List," I have yet to see it. Even in the field of typographical
gymnastics, in high jumping and low diving with twisted brass
rules, I have never seen more elaborate ground and lofty tum-
bling than in a recent specimen that bears his imprint.

It is not to us a pleasure to know that he has practially retired from active business. We need his example in the trade as much as we need his counsel in our meetings. It is a pleasure to be assured that he no longer is obliged to pull the stroke oar of his boat. He has done enough to earn the holiday he is keeping, and we hope it will be long and merry. We welcome him back from his trip abroad.

And now I ask, brothers in our art, that we all rise and fill our glasses and join in drinking this toast: To John Polhemus—the man who goes to the front of the fight, who stays there, who wins. Sunny days, good health, and long life to him. (Loud and long applause.)

Mr. POLHEMUS, the guest of the evening, was given a cordial reception when he rose, and when the applause died away he spoke as follows:

After nearly four months traveling in Europe, I am glad to return to my native land, which is greater than all the other countries I have visited; greater in the intelligence of its people, in its wealth and its resources. Almost everything here is on a grander scale than in Europe. There the old and worthless is conspicuous; while here we utilize all things for the comfort and benefit of our people. Even nature develops larger in our own country than there. Our rivers are larger than theirs; our lakes are larger than theirs; our waterfalls, our vast prairies and fields for tillage broaden out beyond anything they have across the ocean, and we dwarf them by our vastness.

Take all the rivers of Europe and combine them into one, will they make a river much larger than the Mississippi? Take all the lakes of Europe and put them together, will they make one Lake Superior?—and that is only one of our grand lakes. Take all the waterfalls of Europe combined, will they make much more than one Niagara? I never knew before how to fully appreciate my own country, to love it as it should be loved, for its freedom, for its intelligence, for its grand and good homes, its noble institutions for educational purposes, for charities and the elevation of all her people. That great educator, the newspaper, is read in every house, almost by every individual throughout this broad land.

Coming down the East River on the James Slip ferryboat from Long Island City yesterday, I counted thirty-two passengers in the cabin, twenty-nine of whom were reading newspapers. Such a sight as that has never been witnessed in any part of Europe.

In most parts of Europe the masses never read a newspaper, and very little of anything else. Even in the reading rooms of the hotels, if you see a man reading a paper you will find he is an American. We supposed here that it would be dangerous, after the New Orleans shooting of Italians, to travel in Italy. I never heard it mentioned while there, and not one out of every thousand Italians ever knew of that affair, because they do not read.

This year, while the crops of Europe have almost failed, we have abundance. Every section, every broad field, every nook and corner of our broad land is overflowing with a rich harvest.

I will try to be just, however, and tell you in what they excel in Europe. The roads everywhere are almost perfect, and great care and constant labor are used to keep them so. Mostly Macadamized, but in some places paved with stone or asphalt; and in Holland, where there is no stone, they use small, hard bricks, which they call clinkers. In the cities the pavement is without a flaw. No holes, ruts, or uneven places anywhere. I was astonished to find that one-half of London is paved with wood, which proved a failure here, but is a complete success there, being smooth, even on the surface, and durable, and the traffic of London is as heavy as it is in New York, and it is noiseless and free from the disagreeable jolting we are obliged to endure here. Asphalt pavement is also largely used and appears to be very durable. Then the Belgian, or stone pavement, is more even than ours. I account for the evenness and durability of their pavement by the solid foundation they put under it. We have been in the habit of paving in a bed of sand, with only the earth underneath it. They have a concrete foundation from one to two feet thick on which they lay theirs.

I have seen laborers digging in the streets with pick and crowbar, and it was like the solid rock of a stone quarry. This same care in laying pavement is used all over Europe. These smooth, even pavements render it comparatively easy to keep the streets clean, and they do keep them remarkably clean. Boys from fourteen to sixteen years old are employed in gathering the droppings from horses, and receptacles are provided where they are deposited until the dirt cart takes them away. While the streets of London are reasonably clean, they do not compare with the streets of Amsterdam and Paris. In Amsterdam the streets are flushed with water and washed every morning, making them perfectly clean. In Paris housekeepers are obliged to bring out their waste every morning early and deposit it in the gutter; it is then shoveled into the dirt cart and taken away. The water is arranged at short distances to run into the gutters.

and both men and women with brooms wash the dirt into the
sewers.   This is done all over Paris every morning, and done so
thoroughly that the streets are perfectly clean.

I will now tell you briefly how I was impressed with the different countries I visited.   England is first in civilization, in wealth
and intelligence, and London is the center of her greatness.
Her people are as happy, as healthy, and more prosperous than
any other people in Europe.

From England I crossed to Ireland. Here everything changed.
The people are poor, the land uncultivated, except an occasional
patch of potatoes, and begging is common everywhere.   I found
the Irish people, however, kind and very obliging.   They would
take great pains to give information and never refused a tip.
Belfast is the most prosperous place in Ireland, showing many
evidences of wealth and industry.

Scotland was the next country which I visited.   Here I saw
nothing but industry, prosperity, and a high state of civilization.
Great steamships being constructed on the Clyde, all along its
shores, comfortable homes, the church and the schoolhouse, all
telling of civilization and prosperity.   Her mountains are grand,
her lakes are lovely, her cities are solid and beautiful, her castles
teeming with reminiscences, and her old abbeys full of romance
and story.   The city of Edinburgh is one of the most beautiful
cities in the world.

Holland I visited next.   This is the most antiquated and yet
most interesting country in Europe, the land, actually rescued
from the ocean, being from six to eight feet below its level, and
kept from overflowing by immense embankments.   The land is
all meadow land, rich with grass, and large herds grazing on every
field.   It is the very paradise for cattle.   The fields are divided

by ditches or canals instead of fences and all the heavy traffic is done on the water. The public roads are all paved with brick and kept in excellent condition. The farm-houses and barns are large, well built and clean.

The principal city, Amsterdam, consists of ninety islands intersected by canals, and every house is built on piles. The English language is spoken by most of the educated classes, and there are no beggars. The country people, in many places, wear picturesque dresses, the like of which were common probably five hundred years ago. Wooden shoes are common. Industry, honesty and cleanliness are the rule in this country. I saw no cemetery in Holland, and asked the conductor where they buried their dead. He said: "People never die here." That is hardly true. Belgium was the next land I visited. Here you noticed a change. Although Belgium has many of the characteristics of Holland, she also has many of other countries. Beggars and dirt are not uncommon. The cities of Antwerp and Brussels and its battlefield of Waterloo are interesting places. We left Brussels for Cologne, Germany.

Next to England, Germany is the greatest country in Europe. Her people are intelligent, educated, well-to-do, and the Rhine country through which I passed is a very garden of Paradise. From the Falls of the Rhine I went to Lucerne in Switzerland, the land of mountains and lakes, of an industrious but poverty stricken people, full of patriotism and love for their barren rocks, out of which they dig a scanty subsistence. Their women are overworked, bent and old, while still young in years. The scenery is very grand, mountain rising above mountain, many of whose tops are covered with eternal snow, and beautiful lakes laving their bases with their limpid waters. Nature here has done her grandest work in her great upheavals.

From Switzerland we crossed into Italy by the famous Simplon
Pass. I had heard Italy much praised, and expected to find it
beautiful, but was disappointed. I found it hot, dry, dusty, dirty
and full of fleas. I found the people lazy, filthy, cringing beggars, and devoid of decency as we understand it. I never want to
visit Italy again. There are many interesting things to see,
however: its Mount Vesuvius, its Pompeii, its many ruins, dating
back two thousand years and more; churches, chief among
them St. Peter's, the most beautiful and largest in all the world;
its Forum, its statuary, and its paintings. Our guide told us
that the goose in Rome was a sacred bird, because Rome was
once saved by geese. One of our party innocently inquired if
there were many geese in Rome. He answered: " Four hundred and twenty thousand." That is the number of people who
live there.

I have only admiration for France, and Paris is more beautiful than words from me can tell. The people live for pleasure
there.

I spent some days in Paris. It is filled with interesting objects. No place has more that would beguile the time of a
traveler. From France I came to London, when I again saw
some of the things that I had looked at before, as well as many
that were new. No one could understand London, however,
in a visit of so short a time. I then went to Liverpool, and after
waiting some time for passage, was at last able to sail for home.
In my journeys around Europe I had the pleasure of the company
of a number of intelligent American ladies and gentlemen, whose
acquaintance I made on the other side, and I parted from them
with regret. Together we saw many of those interesting and
curious things in which a civilization two thousand years old

ought to be fertile. But, however beautiful or instructive they may have been, I sighed for the country I had left—full of everything that could make life pleasant, and populated by a people in whom the fires of freedom have always burned brightly—America, the last discovered of the continents, but the best, my own native land.

Mr. DOUGLAS TAYLOR, who had recently suffered the loss of his establishment by fire, was called for, and in response spoke as follows :

I am delighted to meet with you, and to assist you in doing honor to a white man. I have taken a deep interest in my friend's remarks. I don't think, however, that while holding such sentiments, he will run for office here in New York, with the possibility of having the Italian vote against him. I see that he has done Europe very thoroughly for the first time, but I want him to go again, and, while not losing his patriotic love for his native land, which seems to predominate over all other feelings, will give us the result of a further and more extended tramp and come back again. It was my pleasant privilege at the last meeting of the Typotheta? before his departure to say a few words, in which I stated that we regretted his leaving, but had a sure trust in his safe return, in his prosperity, in his health and happiness, and to his being with us in the middle of September, prior to going with us to Cincinnati. After his departure we had several meetings, and at the various gatherings we all listened with great interest to the letters in which his travels were related, and while the members had had various and sundry travels of their own, yet through the three or

four months he was away, their " 'arts were true to Pol."
(Laughter.)   They stuck to him, and will stick to him, and this
is a very proper and kind recognition of the feelings with which
we greet his return, a welcome that any one of us might be
proud of.   I, for one, am glad to see it and take part in it.   I
think our President said that many years ago Mr. Polhemus got
burned out twice.   I am trying to imitate him as far as I can, but
I have only got halfway so far.

I am not going to try and make a speech.   Now that Mr. Polhemus is back, we will see him at our meetings and take him to
Cincinnati with us, and there he will refresh all the boys from St.
Louis and Boston and other places whom we will meet with
the story of the remainder of his tramp, which I think he left
unfinished.

Since I saw you I had a disturbance down my way and I had
a great deal of consolation.   Four or five people came up and
congratulated me on selling an old rat trap for fourteen times its
value, and invited me to open wine.   Hearing I wanted to go
into business, one or two came to see me, expecting to take my
little work, valueless as it is, and all said there was a rumor that I
had gone crazy and was about to buy another old rat trap.   When
I said to the first person that that was within the range of possi-
bilities, I got from him a look as much as to say I was a d——
fool.   Then there were the chaps who came to tell me that they
were so deuced sorry I was going to leave the business and leave
my work for their offices to do.   (Laughter.)   I received over
eighty telegrams and messages from people, more or less un-
selfishly telling me to do various things.   Some of them offered
me the use of their offices, and I want to say that the first one
was from the John Polhemus Printing Company.   (Applause.)

That made me feel good, but I had a few people, and I did not want to see them making half time in other shops when I could give them full pay. (Laughter.)

Above all, I thought of the Typotheta. It would seem as if I was going back on my own old society—one of the pet schemes of my life—if I went out of the business. There is no other city but New York, and there is no other place than America. One inch of New York is worth the whole of any other city on the face of the earth, and one foot of America is worth all other lands combined, and I am glad to have our old friend add his testimony to this. The larger part of going abroad is the anticipation of returning home, just as in the burning or loss of thirty or forty thousand dollars by a fire the joy is the kind feeling and hearty sympathy which one meets from his brethren in the profession. Doctors or bankers, or lawyers or any other professional men, may come forward and offer a kindly word to their fellows, but if you want real, open-handed sympathy, go to the printers of New York, as I have. (Applause.) It is my excuse, my family and my friend, and myself in old age, in the sere and yellow leaf, this sticking to the business. I emulate the kind old president whom we lost, the dearest president we ever had and the friend whom we respected. I stay by them and their example, and I am proud to say it here to-night. If I spoke for an hour I could speak in warm tones and feelings of John Polhemus, who would be an honor to any business or any profession on the face of the earth. I feel as if it was my place to say nothing after the eloquent talk of our chairman, and yet I feel as if, had I a thousand columns to write or speak, they would all be of the kindness and warm feeling of affection for him, for you all, for the members of the Typotheta, for the people who telegraphed me from other cities, in and out of the printing business, and I am proud to live and stay in such a business with such men. (Applause.)

Mr. JOSEPH J. LITTLE responded to calls and spoke as follows:

MR. PRESIDENT AND GENTLEMEN: The little notice which I received for this dinner said it was to be informal, and I was sure there was to be no speaking. I assumed, of course, that the president would make a few remarks and that they would call up reminiscences appropriate to such an occasion, but he has covered the whole ground, so far as I can discover, and now I am called to my feet and compelled to reply to aspersions cast on my character. Why my friend De Vinne should refer to me when he speaks of a coach and frills and a colored man behind, I do not know. I have never seen any reason why a printer, provided he is able to do so, has not as much right to ride in his coach as a banker, I have never seen any reason why a printer should be ashamed of his profession, but I have seen every reason why I should be proud of it, and it has been my own endeavor to help it up and give it a better standing than it has sometimes had even from its own professors.

Friend Polhemus accused me of being a deacon. I am sorry it is not so. If it was so I would not be ashamed of it, but lest it might bring reproach upon a profession upon which I would not bring it, I will say I am not a deacon, and I do go to the United Typothetæ. (Laughter.) I must confess I am very glad to be here. It is very satisfactory, as I am reminded in looking on the faces of our President and our guest, to know that it is not so much years as conditions that make age. If we should

judge of the two gentlemen at the end of the table by looking
into their faces, we would think they were of the boyhood
age, and we would bask in the sunshine of their presence and
feel young again. There are a few things in life that cannot be
repeated. For instance, you all know that the first pants we
had with a pocket were the grandest pants ever made. There
never was a second pair so nice as they were. We all know, if we
are married, that the first baby was the finest born. The first
trip abroad was the greatest event in our life. We do not realize
that any other man could have such a trip, with such lakes,
and mountains and Italian star-lit skies. In Italy they have
one thing we do not have here. We do have some star-lit nights
in September, but never has any man in this room seen it equal
to the nights seen in Italy. If Polhemus was there at the right
time he saw it as he never saw it here. [A voice : " He went to
bed early."] (Laughter.) I have explained that I was not a deacon, and I had a right to sit up to look at the stars. I am not
a star-gazer, but I had to see the stars there. The first European
trip is the most eventful in one's life, and I was glad to hear our
old friend tell of the pleasure of that trip to himself. Then
there is another event in our lives. The first grandchild caps
the climax. Our presiding officer was telling about his first
grandchild, and I don't blame him. I have heard that the first
grandchild beats even the first child. I did not intend to make
any remarks, but I am sure you will all join in rejoicing that
the years of Mr. Polhemus have passed so lightly and left him
so free from wrinkles, and will also join in the wish that the
rest of his years —and may they be many — may be as placid and
calm to the end of his journey; and when done with this life, may
he find all the pleasures which await him beyond. (Applause.)

Calls were made for Mr. JAMES W. PRATT, who responded as follows :

I am very glad to meet and greet an old friend after his visit to a
foreign country, and I think we are all happy to be present on this
occasion. Although not born in this country, I was very much grat-
ified on visiting the old country some years ago, to return with
the same experience as that of which he has been speaking. I
was glad to be back, and my comparison with other countries was
the same as his. I did not see anything like this country on the
face of the earth. (Applause.)

Mr. LOUIS D. GALLISON then spoke as follows :

MR. CHAIRMAN AND GENTLEMEN : I do not suppose there is
a man in the room who can say more heartily than I that he is
glad to see Mr. Polhemus back and looking so well. There are
many who have known him more years, but I doubt if there is
a man present who has had so long and intimate business relations with him as myself. Our relations for some ten or more
years were those of publisher and printer. Any one who has
been on either side knows what peculiar relations those may be,
and I have been able to realize since I have been in the printing
business how exasperating I must have been to Mr. Polhemus
in eleven months out of the twelve, but at the same time we
have never had, in all our relations, a single cross word or unpleasant experience. I think that is something remarkable, but I
know it is due to Mr. Polhemus's gentleness of spirit, and his
intelligent appreciation of my ignorance. During his strike I
had large business interests with him, and we stuck to each
other through it all, and came out all right. I told him that as

long as he had a man to stick type I would stay right through, and I did. I appreciated and admired his manliness in holding up to the principle where I knew he was right, and where he knew he was right. I think he did more for the trade than we can realize. It had a lasting effect on the Union, and they do not forget it to-day. I think every master printer in New York owes to Mr. Polhemus a debt of gratitude for his persistence in sticking up for a principle, although he knew it was very severely injuring his pocket. I am glad to know that since then, after it made the turn, his business has been more prosperous than ever before in his life. I hope it will continue to bring in more money for the balance of his life than it ever did before. I am certainly glad to see him, and glad of this opportunity to pay, in my modest way, a tribute of respect and admiration to Mr. Polhemus as a man and as a printer. (Applause.)

Mr. R. H. SMITH followed Mr. Gallison, speaking as follows:

GENTLEMEN: Mr. Polhemus was formerly a member of the Executive Committee, and there is no member of the Executive Committee we are more happy to meet than John Polhemus, and during his absence this Summer you can scarcely have an idea of how vacant our assemblage was. Sometimes we were reduced to Henry Bessey, but we always had Mr. Polhemus before us. There was one feature of Mr. Polhemus of which we had no conception. We knew him as a printer and a hard fighter, and that in antagonism to the Union there was no man like him. All of you know that the Union to him is as the red rag to the bull. He was there every time. But we learned much about him while he was away, from his regular correspondence, which

was always before us, and which we always read with interest.
Why, we had no conception of the amount of poetry there was in
the man. He went to the height of eloquence in his accounts
of foreign scenes, and his descriptions of people put a new
conception on his character. But when he got to Italy it changed.
We were astonished, as we thought his eloquence would then
reach its climax, but he could see nothing in the Italian beggars,
the Italian fleas, and the Italian people. I am sure you will
all say with me, " Welcome home, John Polhemus!" (Applause.)

Mr. POLHEMUS here took the floor, and said :

In answer to Mr. Little I want to say a word. If the Italian
skies are more beautiful than ours I did not see them. They
may be as pretty, but I think the scenery of this country, our
sunsets, and our Southern skies, are equal to those of Italy, or
any in the world. (Applause.)

Mr. P. H. BRESNAN spoke as follows :

I came here to-night to do honor to Mr. Polhemus, probably
my oldest friend in the trade. I am called on very unexpectedly,
and, as I never made a speech in my life, it is rather hard to
commence now. I am here in the hope that I shall learn something from the Typothetæ. I am here for information. I looked
around here when I came in to see how many of our friends
in the same calling were here, and I find I am here alone. It
is embarrassing to be alone. We like to be together. Misery
loves company. Bessey, Pratt and De Baun have been trying to
cheer me up, but I am modest, like any other young man. I am
here to apologize for our trade and its representation among its
friends, and for having to stand here alone to welcome one of
the most substantial patrons and friends of our calling. I have

known him since I was a little boy, and as a man I will say I am proud to welcome him home. (Applause.)

A letter was read from MARTIN B. BROWN, Esq., as follows:

NEW YORK, Sept. 22, 1891.

My Dear MR. POLHEMUS:

I had fully expected to join my friends of the Typothetæ in welcoming you this evening, but at the last hour find myself so oppressed with business arising out of the next election that I am reluctantly compelled to say I shall not be able to be present. But, while absent, I do not desire the occasion to go by without expressing to you my regrets at not being able to shake you by the hand to-night and to say, what every one who has known you must equally feel, that in greeting you warmly we do so as one of the foremost printers of the United States, one of the most indomitable workers that the craft has ever seen, an honorable rival, a just and considerate employer of labor, and one of the staunchest and truest friends ever known to man. You had already attained promenence when I became a journeyman; you were an officer of the Typothetæ before I had gone beyond my first attempts as an employer, and I have watched your career ever since with interest. Our acquaintance began many years ago, and long since ripened into friendship. I trust that this will not diminish as we still further move down on the stream of time, but that it may remain in all its early strength and vigor for many years to come. I hope you will express to the assembled company my sorrow at being prevented from attending the board spread in your honor, and believe me,

I remain, sincerely your friend,

MARTIN B. BROWN.

A letter of regret was also read from Mr. ANDREW LITTLE, as follows:

NEW YORK, Sept. 22, 1891.

E. P. COBY, Esq., and dear friends of "The Typothetæ:"

I am very sorry and disappointed that I cannot be with you to-night; my family had arranged a little affair at Norwood Park for to-night also. I am sixty-*two* to-day—at 2 o'clock, 1829, Sept. 22. I was there at the time, and it is *too* bad I cannot be at *two* places at *one* and the same time.

I trust you will have a pleasant, jolly dinner. You have *the* man, the occasion and the company. No doubt when Mr. Polhemus was "*half seas over*" he had an inkling of this, we will assume. May his embarrassment, coupled with his appreciation, not find him *too full* for utterance.

Believe me, gentlemen,
Yours very sincerely,
ANDREW LITTLE.

A letter of regret from Capt. JAMES PARKER was also read:

NEW LONDON, Conn., September 22, 1891.

JOHN POLHEMUS, Esq.

My Dear Friend: A professional engagement, which has unexpectedly called me here, has detained me until it is too late to unite with your friends of the Typothetæ this evening in giving you your well deserved welcome home. Since 1875, when I, a stranger, attracted by your then well established reputation for prompt performance of your engagements, came to you to ask you to assume the printing of the *Record of American and Foreign Shipping,* neither I nor my successor have ever had any occasion to be other-

wise than thankful to you ; and the result has been the production of a book than which none has ever been better printed in
America.

I shall never forget the cheerful assurance you immediately gave
me after the fire had destroyed your office with the book half
printed (and when I should not have felt aggrieved, had you
succumbed to what seemed a total loss of your labor of many
years), that your promise to have it ready by the time set in our
contract would be kept, and it subsequently was kept almost to
a day. In your case the old fable of the *Phœnix* was realized.

Faithful always to your engagements, both to your patrons
and your employees, you have merited the success you have
won, and the confidence and affectionate esteem which both
classes have always displayed and will, I am sure, continue to dis-
play towards you.

The compliment which your friends are this evening paying
you is prompted only by a warm regard for you as a brother
printer, as a man, and as a friend.

May you live long to receive and to enjoy it.

Yours very truly,

JAMES PARKER.

Mr. WILLIAM CHARLES ROGERS was called for and
responded as follows :

GENTLEMEN : You know I am not a speaker. Your experience
in the Typotheta must have taught you that fact. With all of
you, I am pleased to be here and pleased to add my tribute to the
worth of a good printer and an honest man. (Applause.) If I
had any words to better express my appreciation and love of Mr.
Polhemus than has been already expressed by those who have

spoken to-night I would give them, but I cannot. I can only feel
the emotion, and I hope you will excuse me. I unite with you in
the welcome, and I fully appreciate the pleasures of this evening.
(Applause.)

Mr. W. W. PASKO responded to calls and spoke as
follows:

MR. PRESIDENT: I have been greatly pleased at reading the letters which Mr. Polhemus has sent describing his experience on
the other side. These show that we may know a man, as we
think, very well, but that he may have latent abilities of which
we have perceived nothing. He has been able to give us some
very graphic descriptions of the countries in which he has been,
and of the conditions of life that prevail there, which prove this
conclusively. We have long known him as a staunch supporter
of the rights of those who employ labor, and at the same time as
a friend of those who perform this labor. I must deny that in
his case he has shown any disposition to injure those who are
employed by him or by other persons. His whole history is a
history of the fortunes of a man who has attempted to raise up
not only himself, but those around him. Mr. John Polhemus had
no early advantages in life. His people were farmers. He was a
canal boy. [A voice. "So was Garfield."] He came to this city in
1842, wrought here as an apprentice and journeyman for ten years,
and then began business without money and without any peculiar
advantage that could lead him to success, but by industry, economy and judgment, he has accomplished the things you now see.
In his early years he toiled till long past midnight, and his earnest
endeavors then were that he might be able to get on still further.
How well he has accomplished this design you now know. When

he left Cortlandt street and reached Nassau street, he lacked the necessary means to prosecute his business as he would have liked. But each year since he has added to the things he has needed for his occupation, until at last he has reached the point where he could do what he desired. We are remiss in many respects as employers. We do not add to the stock of materials in our places as we should, but practice an economy which defeats its own object. We are not solicitous enough about having ample materials, and in our use of them we are too often governed by the ideas of our fathers. We do not, then, attain such success as we ought to aim for. Among those who have been receptive of new ideas is John Polhemus. I know and have been told by early printers in this city that forty or fifty years ago there was not a printer in town who had a stock worth more than $10,000, but as time has advanced we have been forced to add more and more until we have come into an equality of condition with the largest offices in the whole world, but while this has been done we have gone beyond all other countries in the matter of improved appliances. I have had occasion frequently to talk with English printers as to what the trade is doing abroad. There is very little progress in the things which we think necessary. Scarcely any dry printing is done there, or in any country except this. They are not taking measures to provide men with the appliances to get out a good day's work. We in New York, and a great many other printers in the country, have added to our stock year by year while trying all new procedures, until we can do far better work than when we began. It may be said that in this city the quality of printing, independent of its amount, has advanced beyond that of any other city in the world. I am supported in this opinion by several gentlemen who have

lately been abroad. We may see in some places a few things done
better than we do them, but take it as a totality it has been im-
proved in this city much beyond anywhere else, and very much
of this improvement is due to the gentleman who sits at the head
of the table. (Applause.) I am delighted that I am present on
this occasion to meet one who has not only added so much to
the history of this city in its printing relations, but who has been
so constant in his friendship, and who has done so much to
advance the cause of labor as Mr. John Polhemus. I am glad to
be here to meet him. No one in this city is more worthy of
honor than he is. (Applause.)

Mr. R. W. NELSON then spoke as follows:

With Mr. Polhemus's remarks as to the advantage of American
production over English I cordially agree. In regard to the
scenery of Europe I am obliged to differ with him a little, especially in regard to the Italian skies, but I was reminded while he
was speaking of visiting the Government printing office in France,
where they employ something like three thousand people, and I
found a department which our friend Bresnan would blush to
enter. They were chopping off the ends of six-to-pica leads for
spaces. The remarks made as to Mr. Polhemus and his contest
with Typographical Union No. 6 struck me especially. Mr. Polhemus's position with them must have been like that of the old
soldier. He had gone through the war, had been called up at
sunrise every morning for four or five years by the bugle, and he
said—as Mr. Polhemus probably said to the Union his great am-
bition was to earn enough money to hire a bugler and have him
play at four o'clock in the morning, and again when he retired to
his couch, and to be able to tell that bugler to go to the infernal

regions. (Laughter.) I am very glad to hear that Mr. Polhemus has prospered more than ever since he released himself from the control of Union No. 6. I had a call a day or so ago from an emissary of No. 6, who wanted to know if I was going to obey the new rules as to machine composition. He presented me with eleven rules. The first was ten per cent. increase on wages on books ; twenty per cent. increase on newspaper work ; ten per cent. in the hours on book work, and twenty per cent. decrease in the hours on newspaper work. Forty per cent. difference ! Under Rule 9, no "dupes" are to be taken or measurement made. He asked if I was going to obey these rules. I said I should disobey ten out of the eleven, and I should advertise for young women to be educated in that line of work. I said that during the previous week I had set over a million ems of composition, and under no circumstances would I again hire any member of the Union. After this, three or four men applied for work. I asked them if they were members of the Union, and when they said " Yes," I told them I didn't want them. They asked : " Because we are members of the Union ?" I said : " Since the adoption of those rules I will not hire a single member of Typographical Union No. 6." It reminds me of the American who was traveling and who had been compelled many times to pay duty on a doll which he had for his grandchild. He had to pay in several of the provinces of Germany. Finally he came to one small province and they said : " You will have to pay a little duty on the doll baby." He says : " No, I won't, I will drive around your d—— little province." That is what I said to the members of Typographical Union No. 6. (Applause.)

The company joined hands and sang " Auld Lang Syne," then dispersing.

To Mr. John Polhemus.

When printers meet their friends to greet
  In fellowship benign,
They fill the glass and let it pass,
  For days of Auld Lang Syne.

     For days of Auld Lang Syne, my friends,
      For days of Auld Lang Syne,
     They fill the glass and let it pass,
      For days of Auld Lang Syne.

We've met about this festive board,
  Where we have met before,
We'll banish cares—a needless horde—
  And fill up one glass more.

     And fill up one glass more, my friends,
      And fill up one glass more,
     We'll banish cares—a needless horde—
      And fill up one glass more.

Here's to our guest, our honored guest,
  May Fortune on him smile ;
May health and wealth upon him rest,
  And joy his age beguile.

     And joy his age beguile, my friends,
      And joy his age beguile,
     May health and wealth upon him rest,
      And joy his age beguile.

MAY 13, 1891.—That splendid steamer, the City of New York, on which I took passage, went slowly down the North River, past the Statue of Liberty on Bedloe's Island, past Fort Hamilton, through the Narrows to Sandy Hook, and out on the ocean out of sight of land. On our first day nothing occurred worth noting. The sea was smooth, the weather just cold enough to be enjoyable, but the ever recurring thought of leaving home and friends and all the associations of a past life, and going far away among strangers, to see strange sights in foreign lands, brought a home-sickness which made the heart yearn to turn back. Far out on the ocean I saw a floating empty barrel, and I was in the mood to moralize. Poor, lost waif, so utterly alone and far away on the waste of waters! How many poor human beings, with aching hearts, feel utterly alone, and far away from home and friends and country! But no more of this. I was just sick enough to decline one meal. The ship made 452 miles on the first day out.

MAY 14.—Second day. Wind blowing from the northeast, very cold, ship rolling, and am feeling very uncomfortable. If I had the making of a world I would omit the ocean. Mr. Chauncey Shaffer said that it was well for us we had none of the "finest" on board, or we would all be arrested for staggering. He is seventy-three years old, and this is his first trip to Europe. There are two hundred Good Templars aboard, so you will see I am in good company; also a large delegation of millers, who were warmly received at the New York Produce Exchange, and will again be hospitably entertained at Liverpool, on their arrival there, by the trade.

The City of New York is a splendid steamer, magnificent in her appointments, and the passengers are making each other's acquaintance and enjoying themselves pacing the deck, watching the sea, conversing, and indulging in various sports. Second day, 468 miles.

MAY 15.—Third day. Bright, clear and cold. Saw to-day, in the distance, the first ship since I sailed. This impressed me with the vastness of the ocean. With thousands of ships upon its surface you may sail many days without meeting one. Marshall P. Wilder, the humorist, who has enlivened many dull hours, is on board, hale, hearty and enjoyable. He will be remembered as being present at one or two of the Franklin dinners in New York.

I love to stand by the rail and watch the sea—the great waves coming from the distance and breaking their force against the sides of the ship, lifting it like a toy on their foam-capped crests. I love to watch its tiniest bubble, and the ever varying colors—blue and green and gray—rippling against the vessel's side, and to watch the horizon, the ship being always the centre of a circle. And how beautiful it was to see the sun go down. Third day, 455 miles.

MAY 16.—Fourth day. Face badly inflamed by the wind, in consequence of which I am staying in the library all day. Ship rolling and pitching. This part of the ocean the sailors call the Devil's Hole, because the water is so deep and rough. Am slightly sea-sick. This in mid-ocean.

MAY 17.—Fifth day. Attended Divine Service in the morning and in the evening.

MAY 18.—Sixth day. Were to have had a concert this evening, but it was postponed on account of the weather and the indisposition of the passengers.

MAY 19.—Seventh day out. To-night we will reach Queenstown. Glory be to the God of the ocean! Ocean without end!

MAY 20.—Eighth day. Landed at Liverpool at 4 P. M., and for a small consideration got my trunk and valise passed through the Custom House, and put up at the Adelphi Hotel. I did not feel myself in a strange land, for everything was homelike and comfortable. The people, in dress and general appearance, were like our own, and on every hand I found politeness and kindness.

MAY 21.—Took the Midland Railroad to London, and put up at the De Keyser's Royal Hotel. Here I met Mr. Hardy of New York and Mr. Hildeburn of Philadelphia, who have been very useful in giving me information. The day I spent in visiting St. Paul's Cathedral, Rothschild & Sons, the Bank of England, Trafalgar Square and the Underground Railroad. St. Paul's is much larger than any American Cathedral. The largest on the American Continent are Notre Dame at Montreal, and St. Patrick's on Fifth avenue, New York. The latter is 306 feet long by 140 feet wide. But St. Paul's is 500 feet long by 180 feet wide. It is 360 feet high, or eighty feet higher than Trinity. St. Paul's was begun after the great fire in London, in 1666, when the preceding edifice was burnt down. It was completed in 1710. The Bank of England is a plain edifice. It was completed in 1804.

In the evening I accompanied Mr. Hildeburn and Mr. Hardy to the Alhambra Theatre. Oh! wicked London! A drinking bar each side of the stage. Drinks and cigars served to the audience during the play, which was of the variety kind. It is a fine, large theatre, three tiers of galleries, and bar and tables on second gallery, where men and women were drinking and conversing. I did not venture higher than that. Sight-seeing is hard work, and I have quite worn myself out the first day. I noticed that the policemen of London carry no clubs, and I am told that they depend entirely upon their strength to subdue unruly men. I am astonished at the number of cabs in the streets; they are everywhere. One I rode in was numbered 16,672. I have been here too short a time to tell you much in this letter, but you will hear from me often while I am abroad. I have made arrangements with the Cooks to start with their first June party. I will meet them at Cork on May 31st, to visit Ireland, Scotland, England, Holland, Belgium, the Rhine, Germany, Switzerland, France and Italy. If I am well and alive I will be home about the first of September.

MAY 23.—Am resting in my room. Find sightseeing hard work. In the afternoon took a seat on top of a stage and rode as far as it went; then on another stage, then on a horse car, then another stage and back to my hotel. Horse cars are of comparatively recent introduction in Great Britain. They had been used for many years in America before George Francis Train, amid much opposition, succeeded in putting one into operation in London. By that means I have taken my first sight of London. The people all seem to be in a hurry, but are civil and obliging. I have seen but one disturbance, and that was two girls fighting with their fists, as men fight. I saw it from the top of a stage. A large number of men were looking on, but made no effort to separate them.

MAY 24.—Sunday in London is a gloomy day. In the afternoon went to church service in St. Paul's Cathedral to kill time.

MAY 25.—Employed a guide. Saw a solid, dismal old granite building covering much ground; this is Newgate, sometimes called Old Bailey. Kept on the outside. Next Smithfield Market, for the sale of meat only. The guide pointed out the difference in appearance between English and American meat. The ice-house turns it pale, while the English has a fresh, red appearance. Next the British Museum. The most wonderful sight to me was the immense library housed under the largest dome in the world save one, so they told me, containing three million two hundred thousand books. The British Museum is not only the largest, but it is one of the most accessible collection of books in the English-speaking world. It has also a large number of objects of art and science. The library is increased at the rate of twenty or thirty thousand volumes a year. How many years would it take a man to read them all? It is full of curiosities of all ages and all countries. Then the National Gallery. Here I saw paintings, the productions of the most celebrated painters of every country, both ancient and modern. Then to the Whitehall Horse Guard, where the Queen's protectors are housed. Next to Westminster Abbey. This is beyond description. Here are buried in the Abbey England's great authors, actors, warriors, statesmen, churchmen and philanthropists. Some portions of the Abbey are nearly one thousand years old. The tombs and statuary crowd one another in every nook and corner. I can only tell you I have been there. A description of it would fill a book. Then I viewed the Houses of Parliament from the outside; also Westminster Bridge and Thomas Hospital. Westminster Bridge was the second of the bridges across the Thames, which is there a little wider than the Hudson at Albany. Originally there was but one bridge across the river, London Bridge, the history of which mounts up to about the year

1000.   Westminster Bridge was begun in 1738, and finished in 1750. It has fifteen arches, and is 1,223 feet long.

MAY 26. — Took the Elephant and Castle Electric Railroad to the Monument of London. The monument, in commemoration of the great fire in London, was erected under the superintendence of Sir Christopher Wren. It is 202 feet high, and has a staircase leading to the top, from which there is a considerable view. Originally there was an inscription upon it, attributing the fire to the Roman Catholics, which occasioned the line of Pope that the monument "like some tall bully lies." By this fire, which was in 1666, over thirteen thousand houses were destroyed. At that time London did not probably have more than one hundred thousand buildings in all. The Elephant and Castle road is far down under the city, and has elevators holding fifty persons to take passengers up and down to and from the cars. It is in some places more than sixty feet under the city, and passes under the Thames River. Saw the Monument of London, the Fish Market and London Bridge. The present London Bridge was begun in 1824 and finished in 1828. It is 920 feet long, and is of granite. Old London Bridge was a very picturesque object, having shops all along its sides. Then down the Thames by boat to the East India Docks. The Tower of London, once a fortress, a royal residence, a court of justice and a prison, is now an interesting show place. Here you can see the crowns and regalia of royalty, the arms and equipments of warriors of the past — a thousand things too numerous to mention. Among historical places is a building once the residence of King Henry the Eighth (now an eating house), where he is said to have murdered his six wives. I lunched in what was once his banqueting hall. Then visited the Zoological Gardens; saw the lions fed. Returned to hotel tired and a little homesick.

MAY 27. — St. Paul's Cathedral once more. I visited Whitley's large stores, where they sell absolutely everything human beings will buy. It consists of a number of buildings connected so that you go from one to the other through covered arches. This, to me, was more wonderful than any of the Museums I saw. Whitley's is still more diversified than Wanamaker's, which is the great American bazaar. Then to the Albert Memorial and Albert Hall, which seats 14,000 people, and has held 17,000. It takes twenty-four horse power to blow the organ. Saw Hyde Park and then to the hotel.

MAY 28. — In the South Kensington Museum I saw a portion of a rotary printing press constructed to print from a roll of paper, invented and built in 1835 by Sir Rowland Hill, which would print either from movable type or curved plates. The newspaper duty stamp prevented its introduction, so says the catalogue. The rotary printing press was slow in coming to perfection. Nicholson thought out the principles upon which it should be constructed in 1793, but never attempted to make one. In 1814 Koenig introduced the cylinder press, and in 1828 the *Christian Advocate*, in New York, was printed upon a rotary press. This press was seen by Thomas McElrath, the late Joseph Sandford, and the Rev. Joseph Longking, who is still living. The column rules were wide, and the columns very narrow, as would be necessary in a type revolving press. A full description of it is in the *Christian Advocate* of that year. Hill again discovered the principle, and about 1842 Wilkinson, in America, perfected plans for its use. Among other contrivances devised

by him to make sure that the letters should not fall out was one
by which a projection at the rear of a type should fit into the
nick of the type in the line before it, thus making it impossi-
ble to slip when locked up. Andrew Little, the genial type
founder, was employed in the foundry when this type was made.
The first machine which went beyond the experimental stage
was that of Colonel Richard M. Hoe, devised in 1847. Bullock's
was originated about 1859.

I notice that all the Museums, and there are many of them,
are free, and they are well worth a visit. Last of all, I visited
the Crystal Palace. The Crystal Palace was originally built upon
the designs of Sir Joseph Paxton, who had constructed hot-houses
much upon the same plan. The World's Fair in London, in
1850, was the first of those great international exhibitions which
brought together the products of every country, and of which
the next will be in Chicago in 1893. The original Crystal Palace
was in Hyde Park, and was much smaller than any of those
which have succeeded it except the one in New York shortly
after, also known as the Crystal Palace. That was in what is
now called Bryant Park, back of the Forty-second street reser-
voir. The English structure was moved to Sydenham in 1854.

To-morrow I start for Cork. My health is reasonably good;
better than I could expect in this abominable London weather.

MAY 29. -- I started from Paddington Station, London, for Milford, and from Milford by steamer to Waterford, Ireland, and
thence by railroad to Cork. On the train I was nearly frozen,
and on the ship I was tossed about by Old Neptune until my
whole nature, and especially my stomach, rebelled. On the train
from Waterford to Cork there was a party of young men and
girls going to ship for America. The parting from their friends

was very heartrending. "Come back, my darling, my Dennis, my darling Dennis, oh, come back," was the wail of a mother, rendered in rich Irish brogue, and with a feeling that told of deep love for the child who was leaving, and of her own broken heart. Thus men and women live and love, and suffer and die, and hearts must bleed and break.

MAY 30. — Took a walk through Cork. It is but a poor place of about 80,000 inhabitants. In front of St. Peter's Market, filling the street, were dealers in second hand clothing; the goods, piled up in heaps, were worn out and fit only for the rag bag. I would not have taken the whole lot for a gift. The River Lee runs through the city, with several bridges crossing it, the finest of which is called the Parnell Bridge. Here, also, is a bronze statue of Father Mathew, the Apostle of Temperance. The most noted place I found in Cork was St. Anne Church of Shandon.

MAY 31. — Cook's party, which I will be with during the rest of my trip, arrived during the night, but I have not yet made their acquaintance. Took a ride through Cork on an Irish jaunting car. Found it an instrument of torture. I think it must have been used in the days of the Inquisition to punish heretics. It is about what riding would be on an angry camel taking short steps. The motion backward and forward, and up and down, worked the legs of my pantaloons up above my knees, and I was very glad when the ride was over.

JUNE 1. — To-day we visited Blarney Castle, five miles from Cork. It was built in the sixteenth century. It rained very hard on our return to the hotel. Blarney Castle was built in the times when Irishmen used bows and arrows. It has its round tower for a lookout, its dungeon under the ground, its judgment hall, banqueting hall, its openings in the walls for its archers to defend it, its battlements on top, and its blarney stone. It is wonderfully old, battered and broken, and would not be worth seeing but for the history of its past, which every step in its winding stairs and every stone in its walls tells to the imaginative mind. Here men from without besieged, and men behind its massive, dismal walls defended it. Here prisoners were condemned to its dungeons and to death. Here children were born, lived their life to manhood and old age, and passed away and are forgotten. These silent walls are crumbling, and the time will come when every vestige of them will disappear, and even its name be remembered no more.

Shandon Church is the oldest in Cork. It contains a peal of very sweet-toned bells, made famous by Father Prout in his beautiful lines called the "Bells of Shandon." The church was erected in 1722.

JUNE 2. — Left Cork for Glengariff, the Irish watering place, where we stopped at night, and the next morning (3d June) rode over the mountains, forty-two miles, to Killarney.

JUNE 4. — Visited Muckross Abbey and Torc Waterfall. You are expected by your fellow travelers to become enthusiastic over every stone wall, tree and flower, or be considered a man without taste. Some of our party were shocked when I called the Mammoth Cave a hole in the ground. "How beautiful!" "Ain't it lovely?" "Grand, magnificent!" are expressions applied to the most ordinary sights. I am disgusted with such nonsense.

JUNE 5. — At Killarney. To-day we visited the gap of Dunloe, Muckross Abbey, Ross Castle, and Torc Waterfall. The Gap of Dunloe is well worth seeing. We went part of the way with carriages and then on horseback to the Lakes of Killarney. The driver told me about a jolly priest whose servant girl left him. He met her one day and said, " Mary, I am glad to see you ; how do you do, and where are you living now ?" She answered, " Indade, father, I am not living at all, I am married." The beggars on the road through the gap, principally girls, followed us for miles, offering to sell us goat's milk and whiskey. At one place a bugler blew a tune, and the spirits of the O'Donohues and the O'Sullivans, who inhabit these barren mountains, answered back in echoes from their nooks and dells and caverns. Then a small cannon was fired, and the echoes hurled back defiance as if challenging England and all her hosts to battle. We had a boat row the whole length of the lakes, and then returned to our hotel tired out. To-morrow we start for Dublin. Dublin is situated upon the Bay of Dublin and the River Liffey. It has many fine bridges, and in the neighborhood are a multitude of beautiful villas. Mountains in the distance lend an air of picturesqueness to the distant views. The White House at Washington is imitated from a nobleman's house in Dublin.

JUNE 7. — Excursion to Ireland's Eye. This is a small island with a rocky projection out of which one of Ireland's giants, at some remote period, took a big bite in order to let the rising sun shine through the hole he made, and this is Ireland's only eye.

JUNE 8. — Visited Trinity College, a fine cluster of buildings, at the entrance of which are the statues of Burke and Goldsmith. Then the Bank of Ireland, which is opposite the College. It was formerly the Irish Parliament House. Trinity College is of the Corinthian order, and three hundred feet deep. It is an imposing building and has a very large library. The Bank covers an acre and a half of ground. The portico, of the Ionic order, extends for one hundred and forty-seven feet. Then Dublin Castle, a lot of old buildings, which, if located in Chicago, would be burnt down to make room for something better. The chapel which is attached to the castle is really a fine work of art. Then St. Patrick's Cathedral, built in the year 1190. In 1865 Sir Benjamin Guinness, the brewer, gave £160,000 to restore its decayed walls. Then Phœnix Park, where Lord Cavendish and Secretary Burke were brutally murdered. This Park covers an area of 1,753 acres, but is not so well kept and laid out as our Central Park. Then Glasnevin Cemetery, where the great Daniel O'Connell's remains lie in a vault, and a monument of granite one hundred and sixty-five feet high has been erected to his memory.

JUNE 9. — Left Dublin for Rostrenor. This is a beautiful health resort situated at the foot of a mountain, "which every one knows was thrown by a giant from the other side of the Lough," so says the Guide Book. Ireland is a wonderful country for giants.

JUNE 10. — Belfast is the second city in Ireland in population, but first in industry and wealth. Belfast has contributed many excellent printers to America. At one time nearly every foreman in large offices in New York was from Belfast. The population of Ireland, as reported by the census enumerators last April, is 4,706,162, showing a decrease since 1881 of 468,674 persons, of whom 3,549,745 are Catholics. This population is about four millions less than in 1840. The poverty of the working classes, the improvident method in which the soil is cultivated and the impossibility of rising above a certain dull level, except by a miracle, has caused a steady emigration from that country to others, principally to the United States and Canada, although the Australian Colonies have received a large number of persons from these causes. Depopulation on a large scale began in 1845, 1846 and 1847, the last being known as the great famine year. From here we visited the Giant's Causeway. This most wonderful formation of rocks by nature is quite different from the idea I had formed of it from the pictures I had seen and the descriptions I had read. The Giant's Causeway is at the extreme Northeast of Ireland. It is about six hundred feet in length, and from two hundred and forty to one hundred and twenty feet in width. It consists of pillars of trap, the ends being at the top, which is elevated above the general surface of the ground from sixteen to thirty-six feet. Each pillar has three, four, five, six or seven sides, although the majority have five, and they join each other as the cells in a honeycomb do, each pillar exactly fitting into the others. It is said that this causeway, or footpath, was originally begun by the giants, so as to extend to Scotland.

JUNE 11. — Back again to Belfast, where we will take steamer for Scotland. Farewell, Ireland,

> " Fare thee well, and if forever,
> Still forever, fare thee well."

Land of beautiful scenery, of hospitable people, of whiskey and poverty, good bye !

Looking back at Ireland, it is evident to me that her only hope is to become in politics and religion assimilated to England. All prospect of a separate government and separate institutions is only in the imagination of the ignorant, and the false hopes inspired by agitators who are not always honest. England, with her immense numbers of people and her great wealth, on whose domain the sun never sets, will not permit three million of discontented people, inhabiting a small island so near her shores, to separate from her. With Church and State in accord with English ideas, Ireland would be one of the most prosperous and happy countries in the world.

JUNE 12. — Arrived at Glasgow this morning. This is the land of industry and thrift. Here, on the shores of the Clyde, were hundreds of large steamships being constructed, and many other industries, giving work to all who want it and are competent to do it. Here I have seen no beggars nor barefooted children, nor men and women in rags, nor huts where domestic four-footed animals lived with two-legged ones in the same room. Glasgow, like Liverpool, has been almost entirely the growth of the last century. Its progress began after the union of England and Scotland in 1707. It not only has a large commerce, but does much manufacturing.

JUNE 13. Visited Loch Lomond, Loch Katrine, thence by rail to Stirling. Loch Lomond is the principal Scotch lake. It is studded with islands, many of them of considerable size and finely wooded, with picturesque shores everywhere. It is twenty miles long and nine miles wide, thus being larger than Lake George or Seneca Lake. Loch Katrine is ten miles long and a mile and a half in breadth. It is confined on all sides by lofty mountains. Stirling Castle is the place of interest here. It would take volumes to recount its wonderful history of battles, of murders, of the kings and queens who have lived there, died there, been imprisoned there and murdered there. Then by train to Edinburgh.

JUNE 14. — It is just one month to-day since I left New York, and this is the first fine day we have had. Edinburgh is the most beautiful and cleanest city I have seen. The drunkenness which prevailed so extensively in Scotland is fast disappearing. A temperance wave has spread over the land. The history of Edinburgh rises in the most remote antiquity, and that city has been regarded as the metropolis of Scotland since about 1450. It is built upon three ridges. It has been particularly distinguished during the last century for its prominence in printing and bookselling, in this respect being the fifth town in the English speaking world, and only being excelled in quantity of turn out by London, New York, Philadelphia and Chicago.

JUNE 15. — Edinburgh. To-day we visited Calton Hill, Edinburgh Castle, John Knox's house and Holyrood Palace; all places of great interest, and full of historical events. Calton Hill is at the East, and a magnificent view of the city is obtained from it. The Castle is at the West end upon a prominence that rises two hundred feet from a level plain. The Castle, with its works, occupies an area of over seven acres. Holyrood Abbey was for centuries the residence of the kings of Scotland. Edinburgh is the cleanest, prettiest and most substantial city I have yet seen. It is built on hills and in valleys, the centre of which, high up, is the castle. Different from most other places, it has a freshness free from decay. The houses are nearly all built of granite; monuments and statues ornament the streets, and parks and gardens at every point, and evidences of wealth and industry are abundant. Sunday is a great day here. Street preaching, processions, and temperance and Salvation Army men and women are laboring with poor and erring humanity in every direction.

JUNE 16.--The ancient Monastery of Melrose Abbey shows many evidences of its former beauty and extent. The arched and carved stone walls tell of an art unsurpassed at the present day, and the old tombs contain the remains of many of Scotland's departed great men. Here is buried the heart of Bruce. Authors have received inspiration from these old ruins, especially Sir Walter Scott, who spent many an hour in contemplation here. Byron wrote the following beautiful lines, which forcibly expressed my feelings :

> " So coldly sweet, so deadly fair,
> We start, for soul is wanting there ;
> It is the loveliness in death
> That parts not quite with parting breath,
> But beauty with that fearful bloom,
> The hue which haunts it to the tomb ;
> Expression's last receding ray,
> A gilded hollow hovering round decay."

The Abbey was founded in 1136. At the time of the Reformation the Reformers destroyed a large portion of it and defaced what remains standing. Indentations are shown where Cromwell's guns battered great holes in its walls. So strife and time have left it but a sad ruin. We next visited Abbotsford, the home of Sir Walter Scott, where he lived and wrote the Waverly Novels. A large collection of arms, pictures, books, rare old furniture and other curiosities collected by him is exhibited to visitors for a consideration. The rooms are kept just as he used them; pleasant rooms and full of souvenirs of great men, curious trophies from foreign lands, pictures and presents. A very interesting place.

JUNE 17. — Back again in London. Here much that I saw before I am viewing again under Cook's guidance. There are many advantages in traveling with Cook's company. You soon become acquainted with the party, and ours is composed of intelligent and sensible ladies and gentlemen from every part of the United States, with whom it is a pleasure to associate. Your baggage is looked after, carriages furnished and hotel accommodations provided. Some of the disadvantages are that you are often hurried from places where you would like to linger, and the route is entirely arbitrary. In hotels you are sometimes given rooms at the top of the building and at the farthest end of the hall. Where there is no elevator this is very annoying. The menu is, in some hotels, very slim. I give a sample below :

MIDLAND GRAND HOTEL, LONDON.

MENU.

Harricot mutton.
Cold meat.
Potatoes.
Diplomatic pudding.

This would be well enough but for the fact that the harricot was insufficient to go round, and the potatoes gave out before half the company were served.

FOR BREAKFAST.

Fried fillet of haddock.
Kipper.
Steak.
Potatoes.

This hotel is owned by the Midland Railroad, and ranks as one of the best in London. I, however, get enough to eat, and am satisfied.

JUNE 18. — A very hard day's work. We walked through the British Museum for three hours, and from there by railroad to the Crystal Palace at Sydenham, where we tarried until ten o'clock at night. The fireworks we witnessed there were beautiful beyond description. The principal piece was a representation of the Battle of the Nile.

JUNE 19. — Visited for the second time the Houses of Parliament, the Tower of London and Westminster Abbey. Saw the tombs of royalty, in Westminster Abbey, some of which date back nearly one thousand years, and only one of the lot has escaped being defaced by religious fanatics. Here Oliver Cromwell was buried. Then his dead body was taken up and hung and then dragged through the streets. Here, Mary Queen of Scots has a beautiful monument. She was beheaded by order of Queen Elizabeth. They both lie very quiet now under the same roof. In the courtyard of the Tower of London is pointed out a spot where many executions took place. Here the guide told us, Henry VIII. had his many wives beheaded. One of our party remarked that it was his divorce court. This is not accurate. Henry only beheaded two of his wives. He was divorced from Catherine of Aragon, his first wife, and Ann of Cleves, his fourth wife ; Lady Jane Seymour, his third wife, died after giving birth to Edward VI. ; Catherine Parr survived him, and the only two executed were Anne Boleyn and Catherine Howard.

London has a population of 5,800,000 people and is rapidly increasing. Its immensity grows upon you the longer you are here, and of the thousands of acres it covers one-third, I was told, belong to the Duke of Bedford. It is inaccurate, however, to give to the Duke of Bedford, or any other landowner, so large a proportion of London. During the reign of the Georges several tracts of waste land were acquired by the grandfathers and great grandfathers of those who now own them, and have since been laid out into streets and houses built upon them. Immense fortunes have thus been acquired.

JUNE 20. — To-day, for the second time, I visited with our party the Zoological Gardens, Hyde Park, Albert Memorial and one of the Kensington Museums. New York still lacks a zoological garden, being much surpassed in this respect by both Philadelphia and Cincinnati.

JUNE 21. — Am packing my trunk and preparing to leave England on Monday night for Holland. I have been pleased with everything here except the weather, which was very bad for the first three weeks, but it is better now. The people of all classes are very civil and obliging. Though the streets are often blocked with drays and cabs, you hear none of the rough language so often heard in New York. The men, women and children of all classes, so far as I have been able to see, are as well dressed, as well fed and as healthy, free and happy as in our own country. The effete monarchies we talk about will not apply to England.

JUNE 22. — This evening left England for Rotterdam, Holland. Found the North Sea a most unpleasant sea to cross. The short waves tried to toss the boat a dozen different ways at the same time, and with fair success. The result to the unfortunate passengers was most deplorable.

JUNE 23. — Rotterdam. My first impression of Holland was rather unfavorable. The people had altogether a different appearance from what I had pictured them, but, after seeing more of the country, I have come to like it very much. Side by side with modern civilization you find old customs, dating back two or three hundred years or more. Strangely dressed women from country places; occasionally men, women and children with wooden shoes; dogs helping to draw carts, so harnessed that the dog is under the cart and the man or woman pushing and guiding it from behind; but the strangest sight of all is a country woman's gold head ornaments, with spiral springs projecting out from the temples on each side of her head. The city is well built, the people civil, intelligent and industrious; no barefooted boys and girls and no beggars, but many of the women have the appearance of having been overworked. They deserve the reputation given them for cleanliness, which amounts to a passion. The scrubbing, washing and polishing the house inside and out which is done here would be regarded as unnecessary in other countries. The country we passed through to reach Amsterdam is well cultivated, the farm houses and barns large, and evidences of industry and prosperity visible in every direction.

JUNE 24.— Amsterdam is a very wealthy city of half a million people, built entirely on piles, and intersected by many canals, which divide the city into ninety islands. These are connected by bridges. Here they prohibit the use of dogs for hauling carts.

All the streets and sidewalks are carefully washed every morning. I asked a man connected with the hotel if he did not think that Holland would some day be annexed to Germany. He almost had a fit. He said, "We have more money here in Amsterdam than they have in all Germany; let them try it, their men are not more than six feet tall, and we can flood the land with water from eight to ten feet. We have only four millions of people here, but we have forty-five millions in our colonies." Here, too, I found the whole people well dressed, intelligent, educated, and an entire absence of beggars.

JUNE 25. — We stop a few hours at the Hague, and then leave Holland for Belgium.

The Hague is where the little queen of twelve years resides, with her court and nobles ; but Amsterdam is the capital and has a Royal Palace. I have searched diligently to find the name of Polhemus in Holland, and have failed. I have been assured, and believe it, that there is no such name among the Dutch. It was a common practice in Holland, Germany and France in centuries gone by to change the common appellations that they derived from their parents for more sounding ones derived from the Latin and Greek. Thus, Melancthon, the reformer, was simply Schwarz-zerd or Blackearth in German, and Desiderius Erasmus was Gerard. The original Polhemus who came to this country was John Theodore Polhemus, or πολεμος, meaning "war" or "battle." He was a clergyman, and settled in Flatbush in 1654. From him all the Polhemuses are supposed to be descended.

JUNE 26. — Antwerp is a very old place, with old customs. Here you see the woman and the dog with the hand cart, the wearing of wooden shoes, but few beggars. I paid a visit to the old printing office, the first ever established in Antwerp, now owned by the city and exhibited as a museum. This printing office is the Plantin-Moretus. It has been described by Mr. Theodore L. De Vinne in the *Century*, and by another writer in *Harper*. A great deal of the material is two or three hundred years old. The stick is on the case, the type is laid, and the copy is ready to be composed, although no work has been done for many years, and little for more than a hundred years. We visited the cathedral, containing celebrated paintings by Rubens. Left on Friday by afternoon train for Brussels, the capital of Belgium.

JUNE 27. — Brussels is a rich and very beautiful city of nearly half a million people. The French language is spoken by all the educated classes, and the Flemish language by most of the lower classes; but many of the people speak both languages. The population of Belgium is five millions, four hundred thousand of whom live in Brussels. The army and government expenses are small, which enables the wealthy people to spend their money on fine buildings and to ornament their public places.

Here we visited the Cathedral of St. Gudule, where for the first time in my life I saw women at the confessional and men in supplication before pictures of saints, earnestly, sincerely and devoutly seeking forgiveness for their sins. This church dates back to the 15th century. Next the Palace of Justice, a modern building of gigantic proportions and bold design. The cost, I was told by our guide, was twenty millions of dollars, and it is not yet finished. Then the Houses of Parliament, which are not large according to our conception of size, but finished with paintings, carvings, mirrors, mantels and bronzes beautiful beyond anything I have seen in our own country. The parks, gardens, statuary, boulevards and private residences are grand beyond my ability to describe. To-morrow we visit the battlefield of Waterloo.

JUNE 28. — We went to the battlefield of Waterloo. Children followed our carriage nearly the whole distance—16 miles—asking for charity. This has become a business on their part, and is the only place I have seen beggars in Belgium. The battle of Waterloo was fought on June 18th, 1815. The allied armies numbered

67,000 men, and Napoleon's forces were 72,000. Not a large number to be engaged in battle as compared with engagements which have been fought since that time; but the issues involved make its reminiscences interesting. That battle subdued a man who had devastated all Europe, and enabled England and her allies to rearrange the boundaries of the nations and compel them to keep the peace. Its influence was felt in every part of the world, and the result brought prosperity and happiness where war and desolation had existed before. The battlefield is now but an ordinary landscape. A large mound of earth has been heaped up at a central point, erected upon the apex of which is a pedestal surmounted by a huge lion, cast from the guns taken in the battle. The ascent is by a flight of stone steps. The Chateau de Frichemont, where so stubborn a defense was made by the English, is pointed out by the guide with many explanations. Relics of the battle, evidently of modern make and "planted" for the purpose of making them appear genuine, are offered for sale in great abundance. For a good description of the battle of Waterloo see Victor Hugo's "Les Miserables."

JUNE 29. — We left Brussels for Cologne, Germany. The Cathedral at Cologne, as you know, is the finest Gothic Church in the world, so I will attempt no description of it. The steeple of the Cathedral, it is said, will be 501 feet in height. The edifice is still unfinished. It is also said that the architect stole his plan from the devil, who had shown it to him in all its beauty, meaning thereby to cause the builder to sell his soul for it. The Church of Ursula has stored in its inner walls a large collection of human bones and skulls, said to be the remains of 11,000 virgins. A ghastly and hideous sight. We were in Cologne so short a time that we had no opportunity to see the better part of the city.

What we did see was not very sweet. A good washing with cologne, or even with clean water, would greatly improve its odor

JUNE 30. — This morning we started up the river Rhine for Mayence, 120 miles from Cologne. I was somewhat disappointed at first, but as we proceeded up the river the scenery became sublimely grand. The terraces on the sides of the hills, covered with vines, the many old castles, the bold and rugged slopes of the mountains, called back to memory the many legends of which I had read when a boy. These Rhine Provinces are the garden of Germany, and have always been coveted by France. Germany will "Watch the Rhine," and only part with them with parting life.

JULY 1. — Proceeded by train to Heidelberg. We are traveling so fast that I cannot see all that I wish to, and do not get sufficient time to write up what I do see. That is one of the disadvantages of traveling with Cook's party. You must follow the guide and the company whether you want to or not. Heidelberg is one of the most romantic and beautiful places in Germany. It is located on the river Neckar, in a valley, and the mountains surrounding it are bold and beautifully covered with green trees. Its ruined castle is the largest in Germany, rich with reminiscences and legends of years gone by, when there were giants and fairies in these old mountains. It was captured more than once by the French and partly ruined, and then recaptured and rebuilt. In 1537 its powder magazine was struck by lightning and the whole building destroyed. It was again rebuilt, but is now a roofless, broken ruin. Here is located the celebrated college where the students drink beer and fight duels, that being an essential part of their education. I saw a large number of them at an open air concert, and I have never seen better specimens of humanity, mental and physical, than these same students. While Germany produces a race of such noble men she need not fear France or any other enemy. The open air concerts here, and everywhere else in this happy land, are resorted to by all classes, both ladies and gentlemen, and much beer and wine consumed; but I have never seen a drunken man or woman, or heard a harsh word, or seen the least disturbance on these occasions. All are well dressed, cheerful, polite and refined, and the music is sublime.

BADEN-BADEN, JULY 2. — This old town was once noted for its gambling palaces, but they were suppressed some years ago. Here men came from every land and staked their money on the turn of a card, generally lost it, and then, in some cases, blew out their brains, thus showing, by their last act, that they had regained their good sense.

The most attractive spot I found in the vicinity of Baden-Baden was the old ruined castle of Hohenbaden. From its elevated position I could see the city and all the surrounding country. It afforded a secluded spot for contemplation. I have heard no legends of fairies and giants, and lovely maidens carried off by gallant knights from neighboring heights; of warriors, armed *cap-à-pie*, pursuing the fugitives and besieging the castle, and how they fought and suffered and bled and died; how the maiden was disconsolate and was confined in a dungeon cell. The castle was destroyed in 1689 by Louis XIV., and the wildness or nature and solitude of the mountains have spread desolation over the scene of destruction.

JULY 3. — We left Baden-Baden for the Falls of the Rhine. Our route lay through the Black Forest, over mountains looking down into valleys more lovely than words can describe. I

was so fascinated that I clapped my hands like a boy and ut-
tered many exclamations of admiration.   The slopes of the mountains, the crystal brooks, the foliage and the vine, and the Swiss
cottages nestling in sheltered nooks, all made a view so beautiful that I said: "This surely is paradise, or a part of the king-
dom of heaven.   Here I would like to live forever, basking in
the sunshine on the mountains, and dream in everlasting peace."
For a description of the Falls of the Rhine I will quote from
my Guide Book:

"Stand for half an hour," says Ruskin, "beside the Fall of Schaffhausen,
on the north side, where the rapids are long, and watch how the vault of water
first bends, unbroken, in pure, polished velocity, over the arching rocks at the
brow of the cataract, covering them with a dome of crystal twenty feet thick, so
swift that its motion is unseen, except when a foam globe from above darts over
it like a falling star; . .   . . and how, ever and anon, startling you with
its white flash, a jet of spray leaps hissing out of the fall like a rocket bursting
in the wind and driven away in dust, filling the air with light; and how,
through the curdling wreaths of the restless crushing abyss below, the blue of the
water, paled by the foam in its body, shows purer than the sky through white
rain clouds; . . . . . their dripping masses lifted at intervals, like sheaves
of loaded corn, by some stronger gush from the cataract, and bowed again
upon the mossy rocks as its roar dies away."

The Falls of the Rhine are about three hundred feet wide,
and the descent about sixty feet.   They are thus of about the
same magnitude as the upper falls of the Genesee, at Rochester,
but carry more water.   They are said to be the largest in Europe.

In the evening the falls were beautifully illuminated, creating
a fairy-like scene, so grand that you feel you would like to live
and look upon it forever.   We had a dreary, rainy, gloomy day
in going from the Falls of the Rhine to Lake Lucerne, at which
place I have finished this letter.

JULY 5. — This bright spot of earth, Lucerne, requires a pen with more inspiration than mine possesses to portray its beauty and grandeur. Here is the old town of Lucerne, with its traditions, its quaint old buildings, its fine hotels, situated on the borders of a beautiful lake, framed in lofty mountains and other mountains in the distance, peak rising above peak, white capped with eternal snow, until their tops are lost among the clouds. Here are rugged, craggy hills, glaciers, ravines and gorges, foaming torrents and rocky labyrinths; all so awe inspiring, so beautiful, that once seen they will never fade from memory. Lucerne is said to be one of the most fascinating places in Switzerland. Its Lion, carved in the rocks of the mountain by Thorwaldsen, its old bridge and its beautiful lake, all induce the traveler to linger here.

JULY 6. — We had an excursion on the Lake of Lucerne, and ascended Mount Righi by a mountain railroad to an elevation of nearly six thousand feet above the ocean and four hundred and forty feet above the level of the lake. How great must have been the convulsions of nature to upheave these mighty mountains, some of whose peaks reach so far above the clouds that from their lofty summits you can witness rain and thunder and lightning below you while you are basking in sunshine!

What a strange people dwell here! So full of patriotism for their loved rocks; who build their cottages, sticking like toys against the mountain sides, in places so steep and far up that the dizzy heights seem inaccessible. What they find there to do, or how they manage to live in these inhospitable mountains through their long severe winters, where snow and storm and cold are so severe, and where the dreaded avalanche so often buries whole villages in its mad and fearful plunge down the mountain, is beyond my comprehension, and yet these people love Switzerland so well that but few leave it, and those that do leave it long to return again. To describe properly the wonderful grandeur of the scenery in this mountain land is more than I or any mortal man can do, and do it justice.

JULY 7. — We took passage on Lake Lucerne for Giesbach. The ascension of the mountain is made by railroad. The Falls here issue from a ravine, fringed on each side with trees, and the water bounds from rocky ledge to ledge down the mountain, foaming, rolling, wildly leaping, mad and fearful in its turbulence, for more than one thousand feet, where it plunges into Lake Brienzeer, and is lost in its calm and placid waters. It was illuminated at night and the effect was fairy like. It required no great amount of imagination to feel that some genii had taken you up out of this world, way up above the clouds, above the moon, far up above the stars, and there, where fairies dwell and sport among scenes too delightful for human eyes to look upon, it had for once been permitted you to behold this beautiful land, and bask in its warmth and bathe in its light, while fairies with gauzy wings and various brilliant hues haloing their angel like forms were sporting for your delight in that wonderful far away. Then, oh cruel fate, you saw the lights go out ; alas, you are back to earth again.

The highest elevation we reached to-day was 3,294 feet in the Brünig Pass ; but the majestic Alps loomed up above us in every direction, while our route led through tunnels, past valleys dotted with cottages and rich with fields and meadows, through avenues of walnut trees and gloomy mountain woods ;

by steep rocks and over swift and roaring torrents; from one grand, imposing view to another.

JULY 8.— We went from Giesbach to Interlaken by steamer on Lake Brienz. The village of Interlaken is beautifully situated in a valley hemmed in on every side with lofty mountains, is well built, and derives its principal support from tourists who, with alpenstocks, with carriages, on horseback and on mountain railroads, explore these regions.

Here we have a fine view from our hotel of the famous mountain Jungfrau, whose highest peak reaches an altitude of over 13,000 feet and is covered with snow the year round.

I have a very poor opinion of the mental capacity of the peasantry of this country. The women are overworked, doing all kinds of farm labor and the children's faces have the expression of old men and women. This is no doubt the result of generation after generation toiling to dig and hew out of these mountain sides and valleys the necessaries of life with so scant a remuneration. The people are poor, overworked and ill-clad, and yet insanely attached to this inhospitable land of mountains and lakes. Switzerland should be, and is, a park for all nations and people of the world.

JULY 9. — We ascended the mountains to view a glacier. The ascent was made partly with carriages and partly on horseback, climbing by a narrow zigzag path about 4,000 feet above the sea. There, in a mountain gorge five hundred feet or more across and fully as many deep, is a body of ice filling the gap, and above that large sloping fields of snow and ice, so high that their tops reach above the clouds.

This was an interesting excursion. The horseback ride, with its dangers in so narrow and winding a path, the clear and beautiful day, and snow and ice in such abundance in July, lent a strange fascination to the scene.

JULY 10. — In company with Mr. Harlan, a young and promising lawyer from Maryland, we drove through the valley of Lauterbrunnen, which is bounded by precipitous rocks, 1,000 to 1,500 feet high. My Baedeker says : " From the rocky heights in the environs are precipitated some twenty brooks, the best known of which is the Staubbach. This brook, which is never of great volume, and in dry seasons is disappointing, descends from a projecting rock in a single fall of 980 feet, the greater part of it, before it reaches the ground, being converted into spray. In the morning, in sunshine, it resembles a transparent, silvery veil, wafted to and fro by the breeze, and frequently tinted with rainbow hues. Even finer than the Staubbach is the Frummeback Falls ; fed by the glaciers of the Jungfrau, the water is precipitated into a round, waterworn cauldron from an immense height, and rushes down with a velocity fearful to behold. During sunshine three rainbows are formed in the spray, one above, another opposite, and the third below the spectator," producing a brilliant spectacle, beautiful to look upon.

During our drive we obtained very fine views of the Matterhorn, the Silverhorn and the Jungfrau Mountains, with their fields of everlasting snow sparkling in the sunshine and elevating our minds by the imposing scene.

JULY 11. — We left Interlaken for Bern, the capital of Switzerland. It is a very old-fashioned place, but we were there only two hours, so I could learn very little about it by observation. It is built on the banks of the river Aare. It has a noted clock tower with a noted clock in it, a bear pit with real live bears in it. It has numerous old fountains supplying small streams of water for the people, the statuary of which is neither moral nor elevating, and a fine view of the Alps is obtained from a terrace in the town.

From Bern to Lausanne, where we would have spent Sunday on the banks of the beautiful Lake Lac Leman, sometimes called Lake of Geneva, had not the conductor quarreled with the landlord, so we take the lake steamer for Geneva to-day, July 12.

JULY 12, 2 P. M. — By steamer on the Lake for Geneva. The Lake of Geneva covers a surface of over 330 square miles, and is above forty miles long. It is thus larger than any of the New York or New England lakes that are not upon the border with Canada. It is 1,230 feet above the level of the sea, and in some places is a thousand feet deep. On the right, going to Geneva, we saw the residence of the Rothschilds, and on the left we caught a very dim view of Mont Blanc, the highest mountain in Europe, being 15,730 feet above the level of the sea. The Lake of Geneva is the largest lake in Switzerland, and deserves all the praise that has been bestowed upon it. Grand mountain ranges bound this beautiful sheet of water, vineyards of luxurious growth are planted on its sunny slopes, and fairest of villages dot its verdant shores. Here, as elsewhere, treasures of tradition and legend, both numerous and fascinating, are told in story and in song for the delectation of credulous tourists. At sunset we had a beautiful view of Mont Blanc. The clouds had all disappeared and rays of light from the setting sun brought it out in bold relief against the sky—white, grand, stupendous. Geneva is well and solidly built, but its uniformity of style in architecture, in material and color soon become monotonous. The streets are very clean, the people civil, sober and industrious, and it is the largest and wealthiest city in Switzerland. Here the river Rhone emerges from the lake and passes through the center of the city with great velocity. Its public library, cathedral, national monument, statue of Rousseau, barracks, town house, arsenal, etc., are all worth seeing, but are too numerous for me to describe.

I will now tell you who the members of our party are, taking them in the order of the list furnished me by the Cooks:

Mr. and Mrs. Wiggin and Miss M. L. Upton, Cambridge, Mass.; Mr. and Mrs. Merrill, Boston, Mass.; Mrs. E. Semmes, Washington, D. C.; Mrs. Ireland and her young daughter, New York City; Miss A. C. Merrifield, Vt.; Mrs. M. E. Morse, Mass.; Dr. S. E. Lawton, Conn.; Mr. W. Beatty Harlan, Md.; Mr. Moses and his wife, Colorado, on their wedding tour; Mr. and Mrs. Bordon, Fall River; Mrs. E. C. Needham, Chicago; Mr. C. DeFebyre and wife, Chicago; Mrs. M. R. March, Mrs. M. C. Ritter, both of Newark, N. J.; Mrs. Frampton, an English lady, on her way to Australia; Rev. C. L. Fry and wife, Lancaster, Pa.; Mr. and Mrs. Dougherty, Ohio, and your humble servant, John Polhemus, of New York.

All Americans but one, and from every part of the States. I will venture to say that no large party ever traveled together more agreeably than ours. I have heard no word of complaint, censure or scandal in all the time we have been together. All have tried to make our journey agreeable.

JULY 14. We left by morning diligence for Chamounix. A very amusing scene was witnessed at our starting for this place. Our conductor is an Italian. He seemed to have some difficulty with the managers of the diligences, but as they spoke French I could not understood what they said. He talked loud and angrily, shrugged his shoulders, raising his arms and hands and leaning his head on one side; then the diligence men would talk back in much the same manner. This lasted for about half an hour. Finally the difficulty seemed settled, and we proceeded on our way through the valley to the town of Chamounix. To describe the journey would be but to repeat the many descriptions of mountains, streams, sunny declivities, wild formations of rocks and scattered masses of stones, roaring cascades and murmuring brooks, ruins gray with age, pleasant hamlets, and an attractive maze of scenery to delight the eye of the contemplative beholder. Chamounix is in Savoy, which, since 1859, has been a part of France. Here we are at the foot of Mont Blanc, and to-morrow we will climb over its largest glacier, the Mer de Glace.

JULY 15.— The weather was so threatening that only three of our party concluded to ascend the mountain, cross the glacier and descend on the other side. Dr. Lawton, Mr. Moses and I obtained each an outfit, consisting of leggings, stockings to draw over our shoes, cheap, soft felt hats, alpinstocks, our waterproofs, mules and a guide, and, after having our pictures taken with the Doctor's kodak, started on the winding path up the mountain. Up, up, and higher up, around boulders, past fearful ledges and frightful precipices we wended our way until we reached the Mer de Glace. Then on foot across this immense mass of ice, stopping often to view the scenery around us and to roll huge boulders down the crevices and listen to their fearful plunge, dashing from one icy ledge to another until they reach the bottom at an immense depth. After crossing this great mass, whose melting is the source of a river, though new formations crowding from above keep the ravine always filled with ice, we started on our homeward journey. First we ascended precipices, climbing through difficult passes for a quarter of an hour, then descended through most frightfully narrow and slippery places, with towering cliffs above us on one side and gaping gulfs below us on the other, where a single misstep would have dashed us down into the valley in fragments before we reached the bottom. Two hours of this hazardous labor brought us to our mules. Riding down hill on the back of a mule is an experience not to be hankered after, especially when, on the brink of a precipice, he tries to scratch his ear with the hoof of his hind leg. Mine was a vicious animal, blind in one eye, and would stop, then start up suddenly with a jerk which would have unseated a novice in mule riding. When we reached the level road I tried to get my blind-in-one-eye mule to ride abreast with the Doctor's, but he would only travel single file. The guide, seeing what I wanted, took him by the bridle and forced him ahead. As soon as he discovered the company he was in he proceeded to eat up the Doctor's mule, which I prevented with some difficulty. At four o'clock we reached our hotel, worn out and wet, having been on muleback and on foot seven hours.

JULY 16. — We crossed the mountains by the Tête Noire Pass in diligences, and then by rail to Brigue, which took all day. Our horses stopped to rest a few moments near the door of a cottage where a fond mother was holding a bright, clean-looking baby in her arms. I chirped at it and it smiled. I then held out my hands, and the mother reached it up to me. After kissing it and talking to it in English, which it probably had never heard before and could not understand, I handed it back. Both mother and child could, however, understand the language of sympathy, which is the same all over the world. The little one wanted to come to me again, and I discovered that babies here can cry in good, vigorous English.

At Brigue the room assigned me at the hotel was on the fifth floor, without carpet, ceiling of pine boards, and all innocent of paint. After a little judicious profanity in the presence of the landlord, I was given the bridal chamber on the second floor, where I slept very soundly.

JULY 17. — The Alps extend from France through Switzerland to the Tyrol, forming chain after chain. They cover an area of thirteen thousand square miles, and hundreds of peaks are covered with perpetual ice or snow. Ice begins at about seven thousand feet elevation, but at eleven thousand feet snow supersedes it. The Jungfrau (Virgin) is 13,730 feet high, the Simplon Pass is 6,579 feet, and the Matterhorn is 12,470. We crossed by diligence over the historic Simplon Pass to Domo d'Ossolo, and then by rail and omnibus to Baveno. Napoleon began the work on this Pass in 1800-1, and finished it six years later at a cost of fifteen million francs. Its object was to provide him with a route by which he could take cannon over the Alps with less trouble than by the Great St. Bernard. There are three other well-known passes, the St. Cenis, the Great St. Bernard and the St. Gotthard. All of them are picturesque. It is a splendid road, winding zigzag up the mountain sides, with grand, wild scenery opening to view in every direction until we reached an elevation of nearly seven thousand feet above the sea, then down on the other side into Italy. Here everything changes. The people speak a different language, have different ways, and are different in appearance.

Baveno is a pretty hamlet on the borders of a beautiful and placid lake, with a good hotel, where we spent the night. The lovely and soothing surroundings of this place invite you to tarry here and " steal awhile away from every cumb'ring care."

Cook, however, has no soul, and we must start before nine o'clock to-morrow morning for Milan.

JULY 18. — We reached Milan about twelve o'clock. It is a city of about three hundred and fifty thousand inhabitants, and its cathedral is one of the wonders of the world, with its fret-work of stone, its many pinnacles and its six thousand statues. Then it has an old wall which is said to have been built by the ancient Romans. It is the capital of Lombardy, and its chief industry is the manufacture of silk goods. Sunday we will spend here and on Monday start for Venice.

JULY 19. — Seven of our party made an excursion to Como and sailed on the placid waters of its lonely and beautiful lake. A thunder storm arose while we were out and all its placidity dis-appeared. This little sheet of water, hemmed in by mountains, immortalized by Bulwer in his "Lady of Lyons," poetized by Byron and others, the admiration of lovelorn ladies and gallant knights, can be as unruly and boisterous as any other lake. The climate is said to be delightfully soothing the year round ; a place in which the weary and troubled may find rest and catch the sunbeams day by day, basking in their warmth and bathing in their light. This enjoyment was not long for us, how-ever ; like the Wandering Jew, we were obliged to travel on back to Milan and prepare to march on to Venice on the mor-row. The Lake of Como will be one of the beautiful memories to talk about with loved ones at home by our own hearth-stone.

JULY 20. — After a long, hot, dusty and tedious ride by rail we reached Venice. To say I was disappointed in the place would not express what I felt. I was astounded. The buildings are old and have a tumbledown, worn-out appearance; the water in the canals is dirty and repulsive; the streets are mere alleys not fit for a cowpath; the people are ignorant and dirty, and the hotels the worst I ever saw, even in Europe. Compared with ours they are but "Hyperion to a satyr," and the odor of the place—oh, ye gods, how shall I describe it? And this the enthusiastic idiot calls "Beautiful Venice."

JULY 21. — In the morning we started out with a guide to see the square of St. Mark (Piazza San Marco), the Doge's Palace and St. Mark's Church. A specialty of the square is the pigeons. They are very tame, and will eat out of your hand. I bought a small package of corn and knelt down and scattered it close by. They gathered around me and ate it without the least fear. This was the most beautiful sight I saw in Venice. In the Doge's Palace we climbed what is called the golden stairs, and passed through the numerous rooms filled with pictures and busts, which are no doubt fine works of art. Most of the paintings are large, showing a conglomerated mass of figures, nude, semi-nude, contorted, in horizontal positions, and at every angle and in every posture the artist could possibly place them, some with that most unnatural appendage of wing which has never yet adorned the human form. No doubt they are high art, and were beautiful in their freshness, and are still grand in their decay, but viewed in the light of history a story of wrong smirches every shade and color in them, and a bloody hand marks every vestige of their canvas. The statuary was too obscene for description, and one room the ladies passed without stopping. What is not fit for a woman to look upon is not fit for a man. There was nothing moral or elevating in the scene, and the whole exhibition is a disgrace to a people who permit it.

We then viewed the Bridge of Sighs, which crosses a canal from the Doge's Palace to the Inquisition, and went down into the dungeons under the palace. They are without light, small, and must have been fearful places to confine prisoners in. I felt a great relief when I emerged from them to light and air again. I saw in one of the rooms a large wood engraving of the world with lettering, engraved by Hagi Ahmed in 1559, and a good impression from it which is framed and hangs close by the original. We next visited St. Mark's Church. They were holding service. The music was excellent, but the large number of huge, greasy candles that were burning vitiated the air to a sickening degree, and the faces of the people present suggested the precaution of keeping one hand on your watch and the other hand on your pocket-book. In the afternoon we crossed by ferryboat to a bathing place on the shores of the Adriatic, where I took a bath in its waters. In the evening we hired music, consisting of several good voices and stringed instruments, and seven gondolas holding four persons each, and had fireworks to light up important points on the Grand Canal and enjoy a moonlight row on its waters. The music was good, and very charming when he halted under the Rialto, the arch improving the sound. All Venice turned out to enjoy a free concert, and at some points crowded us out very badly. When we arrived at our hotel we gave the singers three cheers in good American style, in addition to a pecuniary remuneration.

JULY 22.—In the morning we visited several old churches—with which I am heartily disgusted—then grouped the party into four gondolas and had ourselves photographed. The sun was shining so bright and direct in my face that I was obliged to turn from the camera. I suppose mine will be a very poor counterfeit representation of the original. Then we paid a visit to a lace manufactory, where the ladies enjoyed an hour of blissful delight. God bless them ! In the morning we start for Florence. I have just returned from one last, long, lingering look (and smell) of " Beautiful Venice." There is only one spot like this on earth, and if the Adriatic should some day swallow it up the world would be no great loser.

Our guide tried to impress us with the wonderful sights we were seeing from day to day, the buildings that have stood the decay of time, and spoke of the pyramids, their vastness, stability and grandeur; but I failed to see it as he saw it. Of what use have the pyramids ever been to any human being, and is not that also true of thousands of old buildings in Europe ? Are they not merely monuments of disgrace, and often built by tyrants by oppression of the people ? Are they not ladened with the groans and tears and dying curses of suffering humanity ? True, we come long distances to see them, to see their uselessness and folly, and should profit by the sight and learn to be wise. It is not true that the ancients built better than we do, but the reverse is true. The Rialto is built on piles, but the piers of our Brooklyn Bridge and many other bridges are built away down into and under the water on solid rock foundations. The Auditorium in Chicago, the Potter building, the Morse, the *World*, the *Tribune*, the *Times*, and many others in New York and other parts of our country excel in beauty of architecture, in stability of structure, anything the ancients ever built, and are all used for the benefit of the community. There are no buildings in our cities a thousand years old, and we do not want them. When they have outlived their usefulness, why not tear them down and build what is useful and adapted to the present age ? The present is king, and these dead bodies should be buried out of sight, for morally they are as offensive as worn-out dead humanity. They stink in our nostrils. Did not our engineers construct machinery that lowered Cleopatra's Needle from its pedestal, put it into a ship, bring it to New York and set it in our park ? Had it been ten times as large, means would have been found to move it. As for building a pyramid, why, guarantee a company ten per cent. on the investment and we will build one as large as all the pyramids in Egypt put together—and this is not boasting.

JULY 23. — All day by rail from Venice to Florence, which we reached at seven o'clock at night. Florence is a beautiful city, where many Americans have located to study and enjoy its delightful climate. Here we visited more churches and picture galleries, but as we remained only one day I cannot give much of a description of the place. I will have more to say of Florence at another time.

JULY 24. — We visited galleries of paintings and famous churches, some of which had been built for bath-houses before the Christian era, but the Christians in this part of the world have had no use for baths or cleanliness of any kind since they adopted their new religion. I have heard of priests who vowed not to wash themselves for one year, and kept their vow, and enjoyed it. Florence, however, is a chosen place for many Americans to live in.

JULY 25. — Left Florence for Rome, about which, in consequence of sickness, I am unable to write at present.

JULY 31. — Arrived at Naples. This is one of the vilest places on the face of the earth. I will tell you of some of the things I saw. Fleas everywhere. Women in the public streets examining the heads of other women, and from time to time putting their two thumb-nails together in a suggestive manner. Men in bathing entirely nude and women looking on, and the men would come up out of the water entirely naked and talk and laugh with the women with no visible trace of shame on either side. Children, from the new-born babe up to fifteen or more years old, naked in the streets. Men and women bare-legged and bare-footed and dirty beyond conception. The Neapolitan is an animal, lazy, dirty, ignorant and lousy. The Bay is beautiful, and all the surroundings favorable, except the great heat and wonderful amount of dust, which gives everything a parched and dried-up appearance. From here we visited Pompeii, whose roofless buildings and paved streets have been uncovered after being buried fifteen hundred years or more by the fire and ashes from Vesuvius, which God rained down upon them for their wickedness, the evidence of which is shamelessly abundant in its ruins. And this Christian government of Italy exhibits for pay paintings on these old walls of men and women in beastly attitudes, too vile for description. No matter to what age they belong they should be destroyed, so that they no longer corrupt mankind with their filthy suggestions. Begging is one of the nuisances by which every stranger is annoyed, and only a good stout cane used in a threatening way will rid you from these annoyances. They are very cowardly, with a mock politeness which they do not feel. Like a dog which has been whipped, they will be at your feet when there is an advantage to be gained. After having been annoyed beyond endurance by a lazy beggar trying to sell me a worthless trinket I raised my umbrella to strike him; he jumped aside out of reach, took off his hat, bowed low and said " Adieu, monsieur." I own I dislike the whole beggarly, rascally rabble, who intrude themselves upon us and rob us at every turn. All Italy believes that travelers are meant to be devoured by them, and from every direction they appear at your carriage and beg. Howells says of the Italian character of life : "To make it capable of splendor, but not of comfort; to endear beauty, but not goodness, to the Italian ; to lead him to recognize and celebrate virtues, but not to practice them." Over their squalor and wickedness grand churches are built in which to glorify God, but they fail to improve the morality of the people. It is an accursed land, and I long to be out of it.

JOHN POLHEMUS is a printer well known throughout the entire Union. His short, stout figure; his gray hair and beard, with his youthful countenance; his grave, dignified way of speaking, and his alert movements, are known to all New Yorkers who have business near the City Hall. Only those, however, who are intimate with him know the efforts he has made to elevate his calling, to improve its appliances, and to ameliorate the condition of those who are compelled to earn their bread by daily toil. No man's sense of justice is higher, and none can be applied to more confidently when there is a doubtful question of this kind to be decided.

He was born near Haverstraw, Rockland County, New York, on the 15th of December, 1826. The youngest of four brothers, and losing his mother when only three years old, he was very early obliged to go to work. His first employment was in a cotton factory, and his next upon the Morris and Lehigh Canals, but in 1842 he came to New York to enter a printing office. He soon distinguished himself as a skillful hand pressman. After ten years of hard work, having then saved up a few dollars, he entered into partnership with John de Vries, as Polhemus & de Vries, their work being chiefly auction catalogues. They wrought long hours, frequently not leaving till two or three in the morning, and nearly always staying, when there was work, until ten or eleven. He remained at No. 66 Cortlandt street until 1865, when

the partnership was dissolved, each beginning business for himself. Mr. POLHEMUS removed to No. 102 Nassau street, on the
corner of Ann, where he is now, but his office was much less
extensive than at present. He only occupied the top floor, both
presses and compositors being there accommodated.

In this new place he found an opportunity to carry into effect
certain theories which he had before reasoned out. One was
that compositors must never be permitted to work with scanty
materials. As fast as his means justified, he enlarged and rein-
forced his fonts, increasing them from a thousand pounds to five
and even twenty thousand. This policy he has carried out to the
present day. No one is permitted to pick for sorts, to use wrong
fonts even temporarily, or to adopt any make-shifts. Whatever
material is needed is bought at once. The result was that work
followed preparations for it, until now the establishment fills six
floors, instead of one, and the total quantity of type employed
does not fall short of one hundred tons. Several fonts weigh
each beyond twenty thousand pounds. There are over three
thousand brass galleys, and fifty thousand pounds of leads. It is
believed that this office has more material than any other in
America, except the Government Printing Office in Washington.
In this department, also, he has made many inventions. None,
however, have been patented by him, but all have freely been
given to the trade.

His pressroom is not so large in proportion as his composing
rooms, yet it does a great deal of work of the best class. Mr.
POLHEMUS is one of the very few employers who are practical
power pressmen, and he is thus enabled to exercise an intelligent
oversight over this branch of his business. A few years ago he
added a stationery store, which is a large and well stocked one,

Its specialty is law blanks, which are published by him. They cover everything required in the New York and New Jersey Courts, or in Federal practice.

To three classes of work Mr. POLHEMUS has always paid attention. Law cases and law work generally is the first, though not the most important. Cases which do not extend beyond a thousand pages are all put up at once. Newspapers and periodicals have formed a great portion of his labors, but the part of his office which is most nearly unique is that where tabular and statistical work is done. His extraordinary fonts of capitals, figures and points enable the most difficult work to be executed at once. These peculiarities caused him to be chosen by Governor Tilden to print the figures exposing the Ring frauds, and by the New York *Tribune* to set up the supplement containing the Beecher trial. Another extraordinary feat accomplished by him was printing Goulding's New York Directory, embracing over nine millions of ems, in eleven days. This has never been equaled for speed.

Mr. POLHEMUS has been a member of the Typothetæ from its beginning, in 1863, until the present time. He has been a member of its Executive Committee, and was lately its chairman, vacating that office to become treasurer. He has frequently taken part in its conferences with journeymen, representing the views of the employers with dignity and ability. He was a delegate to the national conventions of the Typothetæ at Chicago, New York, St. Louis, Boston and Cincinnati, but was prevented from attending the first by the state of trade in this city. He was present at the next meeting here, where he was the most active of the Entertainment Committee. When he went to St. Louis he made an extended tour through the South and West. In each of these conventions he took a leading part.

He is always on hand at his office by eight o'clock, and does not leave till after five, putting in a full day's work. For the last twenty years he has lived at Flushing, ten miles from New York, where he has a very pretty home. He was married forty-four years ago to Miss Elizabeth Blackledge, whose loss was deplored by a large circle of friends, and their union was blessed by three children. His youngest, a very affectionate daughter of high artistic promise, whose work decorates his entire house, died eight years ago.

Mr. POLHEMUS, it might be added, is very sturdy and energetic, and, in consequence, is generally successful in anything he undertakes which he believes to be right. An example of this is shown in his dealings with Typographical Union No. 6. Up to 1887 he employed Union hands exclusively throughout his establishment, and all the demands of the Union were conceded by him. When these, however, went beyond what Mr. POLHEMUS thought was right, he refused any longer to yield and made his place independent. He now refuses to recognize the Union in any shape whatever, his business never being more prosperous than it is at present.

Mr. POLHEMUS has undeniably and deservedly earned the proud position he occupies to-day as one of the foremost of living printers. In the fact that he is himself a thoroughly practical craftsman undoubtedly lies the secret of his success. Assiduous personal supervision was of primary importance in building up his business a quarter of a century ago, and while now full of years and honorable gray hairs, his business acumen shows no signs of decay. He is of Dutch stock and is proud of the distinction, and does not often lose the opportunity of impressing that fact upon his visitors. He is hale and hearty, as well as bright and cheerful, and commands the respect and confidence of all his business and social acquaintances.

His relations with his employees are of the most cordial character. He knows and understands them, sympathizes with their misfortunes, and rejoices in their good luck. This epitome of his business career demonstrates what singleness of aim and indomitable perseverance, combined with a high standard of moral rectitude, are capable of achieving in the course of half a century of business life. But this tireless worker has not yet finished his course, and it is hoped and believed that many more years of successful life and of ease are yet before him.

W. W. PASKO.

www.ingramcontent.com/pod-product-compliance
Lightning Source LLC
Chambersburg PA
CBHW032353020726
47499CB00008B/2724